# GALAHAD

THE PENINSULA PRIZEWINNING NOVEL

# GALAHAD

PAUL NEWMAN

HALSGROVE

In association with the

𝔚𝔢𝔰𝔱𝔢𝔯𝔫 𝔐𝔬𝔯𝔫𝔦𝔫𝔤 𝔑𝔢𝔴𝔰

First published in Great Britain in 2004

British Library Cataloguing-in-Publication Data
A CIP record for this title is available from the British Library

ISBN 1 84114 348 0

HALSGROVE

Halsgrove House
Lower Moor Way
Tiverton, Devon EX16 6SS
Tel: 01884 243242
Fax: 01884 243325
email: sales@halsgrove.com
website: www.halsgrove.com

Printed and bound in Great Britain by Cromwell Press, Trowbridge

# CONTENTS

*To Pam who urged me to write this book*

# fOREWORD

My name is Galahad.  This is my story, and I swear by the Holy Rood it is all true.  I am known as a knight of Arthur's court, sinless and without mortal blemish – a reputation you may well question after reading what I have set down.  This books deals not only with my boyhood, but with the troubles and tournaments of my middle years, my amatory exploits, ambitions, failures and quest for the Grail.  Handwritten, on costliest vellum, when read aloud, this book should appeal to all, from swineherds to archbishops.

# ACKNOWLEDGEMENTS

Arthurian lore incorporates anachronisms as well as diverse strands of influence as this does this work of fiction. Readers may pick out borrowings and adaptations from Shakespeare, Mallory and Chaucer as well as works like *The Golden Legend*, *The Mabinogion* and the *Gesta Romanorum*, often employed as a motif to kick-start the action. All these sources I gratefully acknowledge.

# fLOOD

I am standing in the corner of a lofty timber hall, listening to my father, the Court Baron, as he administers justice to serfs and tenant farmers. In the obscure hamlet of Dykesyat, the felonies are of no great import: a choked ditch, illegal eel-traps, a broken hurdle, an impounded pig or a lost sheep.

Father sits on a carved wooden chair. The peasants squat on the rushes strewn at his feet, attending with grim, passive looks to his rulings and sentences. The hall is lightless and smells of old meals and smoke. A high wind has been sweeping across the flats all day, making the rafters creak and strain.

I gaze around at the company. The summer heat has scorched their necks scarlet and many of the serfs are marked by the pox. Ill-clad in coarse grey-blue worsted cloth, they are all of different shapes and sizes, like turnips grown on stony ground.

'Simon Gunthorpe,' my father says, 'you have a complaint to lodge against Lob Peters for unlawfully laying eel-traps on your land.'

Silence – a rush of cold wind blows into the hall. I sniff it and sense a strangeness there. It does not smell of hay-ricks and sweating hedgerows. The odour of salt is laden on its wings and I think of distant shores and tall cliffs.

'Father!' I shout.

My warning is lost in the commotion that follows. A long tongue of murky water gushes through the open door, fans out and surges around our feet. The next moment everyone is running around thigh-deep in it, and fighting to get out.

'The sea-walls have been breached,' a man cries. 'All the pasturage has been tainted.'

The warning flares out – but I cannot act on it! For I am knocked back by a roll of water that sweeps over me in a shattering throng of bubbles, and I am under it, in a drowned world, choking and hearing shouts and juddering echoes from above me.

Taking high, plunging steps, Father struggles to reach me. He scoops me up with his arm and hoists me upon his shoulders. Then he breasts across the swirling water towards the bright arch of light which marks the open door. Amid a turmoil of voices and hacking arms, he bludgeons his way. He reaches the entrance and breaks into the outer world. The wind strikes fresh on our eyelids and cheeks. We draw it into our lungs and gaze with startled eyes.

'By Providence!' Father exclaims.

It is a different world. No fields, no hedgerows or ditches are visible. Only acres of grey water with the sombre sheen of old armour. Shock-heads of willows and thatched roofs pierce the metal skin and dominating all is the Tor of Glastonbury like a faery island crowned by the small grey tower of an ancient house of worship. On a small hillock beyond the flour mill, peasants have gathered to escape the rising waters. Lower down, terrified cattle are blundering and rampaging, trying to escape the huge shield of liquid rippling around them. Rats and mice are clinging to the drenched fleeces of sheep who stretch their necks and cry in vain.

The serfs have now shouldered their way out of the hall. They launch themselves upon the tide and begin swimming, making towards the hillock where the rest are gathered. Spluttering and splashing, they curse hapless fortune which crushes the poor underfoot. As for Father, he does not even deign to move but stands waist-high in the water appraising the devastation. With his mouth drawn and his eye stern as a raven's, he watches milking stools, tables and bird-cages float past upon the tide. Then comes a whole flotilla of delighted goslings, better adapted to the change. A number of gulls have strayed in with the flood; they cry and weave the wind as they hover over their extended dominion.

The water showing no sign of abating, Father wades over to a tall elm and heaves me up. Gripping a lower branch, I lever myself into place. Whereupon he comes up and joins me, and breathing tightly, we watch from the safety of the treetop. Not understanding what it all means, I prattle on happily; to me the flood is like a sudden snowfall, a marvellous visitation, not a catastophe which renders useless a year's hoeing, draining and cultivating.

'Now we have this big lake, Father,' I say, 'will you make me a boat? Then I can go fishing with Stephen Gyler.'

'Do not make light of this, my boy,' he replies. 'Men will suffer and starve as a result.'

A solemn pause then I ask, 'Why did it happen father?'

'Hundreds of years ago,' Father says, placing his arm around me, 'we snatched this land from the sea. We held it back with dams and ditches and drained and cultivated it. But the battle was close-fought and the memory of the tide is long. Like a famished wolf, it has waited and watched. And now, at the time of the round moon, it has bared its teeth. It has returned to stake its claim once more.'

I nod my head but do not understand. We wait balancing on the broad boughs until the wind drops and no more waves follow up behind. The current slackens; the ripples flatten and disappear. Rows of willow come into view, trailing festoons of weeds like ragged green hair. Stone-built byres and dovecotes resume their squat shapes, but the straw-and-clay mortar binding the walls of the peasants' huts has been impaired, leaving sodden humps instead of habitations. Finally, with much gulping and snorting, the water slinks back to the marshes and estuaries. The tips of flattened grass-blades begin to appear, and my thoughts of owning a boat recede. Instead I am left inhaling salt and mud smells and looking at immense glistening sheets and pools and slimy fields that have lost their summer lustre.

'Wait here, my son,' says father, slipping off his perch. 'I will come back for you later.'

Climbing down from the elm, he sloshes across to the stables and attends to the terrified horses. Several have died of fright, but he finds one that he can saddle and mount. He rides back upon it to the manor house, situated on low ground beside the meadows of the Brue. At the gateway his serving-man importunes him. 'My Lord,' he cries. 'I have bad news for you. Your good lady was drowned in the flood.'

# DYLFRIC

Mother dead: a hump of earth, an engraved stone, a memory vibrating amid the hollow spaces of air. Whither had she gone? Where could I find her save in dreams and thoughts of the past we had once shared? How much keener is an absence than a presence! Gone forever – what a long word to roll on the tongue. Forever. It stretched over horizons, hills and mist-bound seas. It glittered and shivered and left me beached on the shore of its emptiness. Like most sons, I had taken my mother for granted. It was her job to administer warmth and consolation, whatever the temper of my mood. Yet I had been selfish and unaware of her needs. And I recalled how she had smoothed away life's knottier surfaces, made things appear easy when they were not, and now, unprotected, I had to take the knocks and blows myself, to learn what it is to be a free-standing person without a mother always interceding between oneself and the world.

Father, too, was heartbroken. But he had to maintain a dignified front. The offspring and wives of several high-ranking families had also been claimed by the deluge. Three days later he attended mother's funeral, and then he rode out to supervise the rebuilding of the sea-defences at Highbridge. When he returned, he told me that he intended to renounce his former life of hunting and hawking and devote the rest of his days to religion. The first thing he did was to honour mother's memory by having a chapel erected on Dorville's Hill, a high place and safe from any further encroachments of the tide. 'Your mother cannot be here as a person,' he told me, 'and monuments and statues amount to little more than vainglorious boasts. But if you build something that can be used – a shrine or hermitage – then her memory will be kept alive by the ever-burning flame of piety and devotion.'

So he contacted the abbot of Glastonbury and asked if he knew of an anchorite desirous of a hermitage amid the flats. Promptly the abbot dispatched a monk called Dylfric, a man who had already achieved some reputation for curing the knight Drogo de Nunci of paralysis.

Aged twelve at the time, I was trying hard to conceal the deep sense of loss I felt at my mother's death with unruly, wayward behaviour. Nor was I enamoured when I first set eyes on Dylfric. He was prune-faced and wizened and seemed to be suffering from a perpetual cold. But he was quick to harden into the mould of resident holy man. He applied himself to the role with punitive fervour. Throughout the long hours of frost, rain and sunshine, he sat and shivered, grumbling prayers, like a man who had nothing else to do, which I suppose he had not.

That summer my father hired a new serving wench called Amelia to take on the extra household duties. Also, he paid a woodcarver to build a second shrine to honour mother's memory, a wayside cross beside Dunkerton Bridge on Martin Street. One morning Amelia, who was big, cheerful and slow of tongue, was coming down from the flour mill and over the bridge. Stopping, she picked up a few flowers, knotted them in a posy, and set them down at the base of the shrine. She knelt and mouthed a silent prayer, her lips moving at first gently then more rapidly, eventually writhing and snarling and bubbling spittle. She stood up and began to shiver like one afflicted by a terrible chill, and then she bowed over and took the weight of her body on her hands. Kicking her woollen-clad legs into the air, she balanced on her head, grimacing as her skirts fell back and lapped around her chin. All the while going through these motions, she cackled and whooped like a fiend.

The clerk who lived by the bridge saw Amelia's strange turn of behaviour through the window of his cottage. He mounted his horse and rode down to the manor and knocked on our door.

Father had been supervising the building of a new dovecote; he answered the door with feathers clinging to his jerkin.

'Your serving-woman is acting as if she has lost her wits,' the clerk told him. 'Look, her privy parts are on display.'

Father gave a look of sombre distaste. Leaving his work, he accompanied his informant up to the bridge. There he observed Amelia's postures with a mixture of fascination and disgust.

'The wretched girl is possessed by demons,' he said sternly. 'We will have to prick her or duck her.'

'Why not take her to Dylfric?,' the clerk suggested. 'He is reputed to be skilled at banishing evil spirits.'

The following morning Father and I tramped up Dorville's Hill. We reached the tiny snail-shell of a chapel, too short to lie down in and too low to stand in. Outside was the anchorite, Dylfric, kneeling on a smooth stone slab and praying. His look was one of dour determination rather than religious ecstasy.

'Truly, a holy man,' my father observed. 'Look at his sores. By God, there's a running ulcer on his shin! Heaven will find a place for him.'

'Give me a sign O Lord,' muttered Dylfric, becoming aware of visitors.

There was a dull rumble of thunder followed by a crackling in the air. A fork of lightning nerved its way down and a swash of rain pelted us briefly then departed.

'He does not care about the rain or lighting,' Father went on, patronising the current fashion which read all manner of spiritual merit in bodily abuse. 'He hears the voice of God in celestial eructations.'

Father stepped towards Dylfric, head bowed and hands clasped. But his deferential posture made no impression, for he was stopped in mid-step by the unexpected appearance of another.

It was not a gradually growing presence so much as a manifestation – a loud shout of arrival. A man seemed to leap above the skyline, a tall, lumpy figure coming up from the other side of the hill. Taking long, jubilant strides, he devoured the long grass. His upper half was rigid as a tree-trunk while his legs seemed active as scissor-blades. His coarse round face, topped by a scrawny tuft of hair, brought to mind a large onion. He had blunt and basic features with a hook nose and eyes that burned with a strange and stubborn enthusiasm.

'Are you the anchorite, Dylfric?' he called to the crouched figure praying in the rain. 'The one who cured the knight whose legs had gone stiff?'

The voice had a primitive authority that whittled whoever it addressed down to the size of its needs.

Dyfric bristled at the interruption and then sneezed affirmatively.

'Yes, I was able to ease his condition.'

'Well, I wish you to cure me.' The man threw off his cape. He had a long knobbly legs, a broad barrel chest but no arms, only strangely prominent shoulder blades like twin humps.

'Tell the Good Lord to grant me a pair of arms like any other man. I was born bereft of them.'

Dylfric frowned. 'I cannot do that. God intended you to have no arms, else he would have fitted you with them.'

The man's face darkened. Lifting up his right foot, he bent it back with remarkable pliancy and shook it in Dylfric's face. 'If you do not heal me,' he growled, 'I will give you a good basting. And that will be as the good Lord intended, else he would not have allowed me to get this far in the first place.'

'What do you need arms for?' Father interrupted. 'You seem to have admirably remedied the defects of nature by using your feet with such dexterity.'

'I wish to get married,' the man replied. 'But men mock me – say I'm ugly but 'armless.'

'Indeed,' said Dylfric. 'You must ignore the taunts of the unlearned. The lion, the king of beasts, has no arms. Yet he is in no way defective as a husband.'

'But he has legs.'

'Exactly!' said Dylfric. 'And so have you. Now don't shake your foot at me. Let me be of help instead. God has something for everybody. If it's marriage you're thinking of, I have here a bit of bedstraw from the mattress of St Bridget.'

The armless man looked sullen yet curious. 'What will that do?'

'It will make you an effective husband by increasing your virility.'

This remark seemed inspire him. 'I shall become a lion among men.' He gave a smile like one of those doltish grins cut in pumpkin lamps, then arched his body over and essayed an improbable roar.

Dylfric forced an indulgent smile. 'Yes, it will make you feel proud and capable as lion. It is only five coppers. Can you afford that?'

The man abandoned his beastly caperings and stood up straight. He nodded at Dylfric then bent his leg upwards, arched his foot with amazing agility, letting the toes dip into his baggy waist pocket. He removed five coins with beaming assurance and transferred them to the prim palm of Dylfric.

'Off with you now, man!' said the anchorite counting the pennies, 'Pray twice daily, at morning and eve, and be sure that you make a good husband. Who is the bride, by the way?'

The man wrinkled his nose at the question.

'Why do you ask?'

'I merely wondered,' replied Dylfric, 'who she was. A lass who toils in the fields? An apple picker or cowgirl?'

'No, she is none of those,' the man declared.

'Who is she then?'

The man took a deep breath, as if he needed to puff himself with up courage in order to broach the matter, and replied.

'I do not want to tell you, but I will only say she is a figure of repute.'

'Repute?' echoed Dylfric, with a dry chuckle. 'Truly man, what is your secret? Are you marrying someone of royal blood?'

'No, she is of common stock but very holy – holier than you, in my opinion.'

Dylfric squeezed up the lids of his eyes. He looked like a large, angry mole. 'What are you talking about, man? Who around here is holier than me?'

The man hung his head resentfully. 'I will not say, for it is not your business.'

'It *is* my business,' said Dylfric. 'I am the shepherd of all souls with whom I come in contact.'

Father nodded approvingly – he was impressed by such phrases – but the armless man was angered. 'No, it is not *your business*!' he nearly shouted. 'It's nobody's business, only Elfrida's and mine!'

At this Dyfric's neck thrust out like a swan warding off an attacker.

*'Elfrida – did I hear you say Elfrida?'*

'Yes,' replied the man, standing his ground. 'I am marrying St Elfrida of Taunton.'

It was a plain enough statement. But Dylfric appeared to be having great trouble digesting it. There was a stunned pause during which he stood facing the man, his lips moving in soundless indignation. His gaze contracted until his pupils were dark dots of resentment. 'St Elfrida!' he exclaimed. 'Fie – shame on you! May God punish you for your blasphemy!'

'Tis true,' said the man drolly. 'St Elfrida and I are going steady. We are shortly to set up home together. We shall be snug as peas in a pod.'

Dylfric swallowed hard and clenched his fists. 'What a monstrous slander!' he cried. 'I know St Elfrida – a beautiful, holy virgin who's heals the sick, baptises the heathen and performs countless miracles. Not only is she learned, she has a divine singing voice and her needlework is beyond reproach. It is utterly beyond belief that she would take up with the likes of you. Never! For she spurns the snares of the sensual world – she holds to vows of chastity and obedience!'

'Ah, that was before I told her that I loved her.'

'Pray do not pollute my ears with more of your vile imaginings!'

Dylfric turned away.

But the man was proud and cocky now. He puffed out his chest and nudged the anchorite's back with the tip of his nose in order to recall his attention. 'Listen, I shall tell you how it all came to be. I had spent a morning picking worts on the Quantocks, when it began to rain, and I sought refuge in the chapel at Goathurst. There I found Elfrida, kneeling before the altar, praying to the image on the cross. Tears were streaming down her cheeks, for she was grieving over Our Lord's agony. I crept up behind her and knocked the cross off the altar, saying, 'Don't worry about him – he's a dead duck, while I'm a warm and living man.' And then, running my toe all the way down her back, I whispered, 'Elfrida, you're a fine strapping lass, and I am going to make you a proud and happy mother.' And before you could say Our Father, I had pushed her up against the chancel arch and was raining hot, wet kisses on her lips.'

Dylfric retreated at this disclosure. When the armless man went after him, he made a nervous waving gesture. 'I do not believe it – an impious falsehood!'

'Tis true as Our Lord came to Glastonbury,' said the man. 'And now, thanks to you, kind holy man, I know that I did right. For I am like a lion, the king of all beasts.' Opening the scarlet hatch of his mouth, he let out another exuberant roar. Ignoring such taunts, Dylfric went back to his meditation slab. Sticking his nose in the air, he knelt and began to pray with studied determination.

Turning, the armless man gave Father a conspiratorial wink. 'There's no bride hotter than one that's just quit a nunnery. All that prayer and penitence, it keeps 'em on the boil.'

Father received the tidbit of personal philosophy with a frown. Whereupon the armless man, giving a farewell flourish of his sole, walked away and began to descend the hill.

We waited until the aimable deformity had passed out of sight. Then, with rather stiff politeness, Father went over to Dylfric, saying. 'We have a problem down in the village.'

Dylfric took a sharp sniff, which was his way of telling my father to continue.

'Our serving-girl is afflicted by demons. Could you minister to her?'

Dyfric asked. 'Does she vomit toads and snakes?'

'Nay,' Father replied, 'her table manners are excellent. But she does foam at the mouth and hurl her body about.'

Dyfric nodded. 'I will call tomorrow.'

The next day he came down to our farmhouse holding a Bible. Father took him into the scullery and introduced him to Amelia who was stout and sturdy with calm bovine eyes. Shyly she smiled at the anchorite and curtsied. 'If you show her a crucifix,' my father told him, 'she will demonstrate her sickness.'

Dylfric took out a rosary from his cloak and held the cross over Amelia's forehead. Whereupon she began to snarl and foam and enact the most remarkable acrobatics, including thrusting her head between her legs and standing on her head and dropping her legs back so that her toes touched her ears.

The anchorite appraised the gyrations critically. He then stroked her chin, saying, 'Definitely the Devil has got inside her.'

Father asked. 'What shall we do?'

'We could,' Dylfric replied, 'charge the Devil to depart from her in the name of God and trouble her no more.'

Father nodded.

'But I think I have a better idea,' said Dylfric decisively. 'Next Tuesday, let us all go along the Harrow Way to Yardley.'

Father looked surprised at this suggestion but did not question Dylfric's authority. On Tuesday morning we got the horses ready and took the road to Yardley. Amelia seated herself dumb-eyed in the cart beside my father and Dylfric. It was high summer and the anchorite glared at the buzzing hedgerows, as if all the blossoming flowers were a vulgar affront, while Amelia grinned, waved and pointed at the birds and butterflies.

At Yardley we tethered the horses and cart and went across the fields to the site where the great country fair was in progress. Wool merchants were there in plenty, selling their druggets, serges and baizes, and there was a fine show of sheep and cattle. But it was the competitive activities that seemed to interest Dylfric. He took us past men chasing greased piglets and others engaged in cudgel-playing and wrestling, until he reached a small roped-off area where a little man with ginger hair was seated on a stool sucking a straw.

Dylfric tapped him on the shoulder. 'Is this where the tumbling contest takes place?'

The man nodded. 'In the afternoon. You wish to enter?'

'Nay,' said Dylfric. 'Such frivolity is beneath me. But I have a wench here who is desirous of showing off her skills.'

The afternoon went on and many people gathered to see the tumbling. Father appeared increasingly puzzled and concerned. Dylfric was busy supervising Amelia, urging her for modesty's sake to wrap some coarse brown cloth around her flanks. 'Otherwise lewd eyes will spy on you,' he warned.

This puzzled us further but we hung around the arena. We watched a man juggling eggs and balancing a swede on his nose at the same time, followed by another fellow who got badly clawed riding a bear. Then it was time for the prize performers who demonstrated the latest rolls learnt from the jongleurs and acrobats of the Continent. Finally it was Amelia's turn. As she was the only female entrant, her appearance sent the crowd into raucous hoots and cheers.

Like a big nervous calf, Amelia stepped into the circle, her face mutely protesting at the indignity. But then Dylfric lifted his crucifix and thrust it towards her. Her eyes lost their credulous open gaze, became small and intent as they fixed on the cross. Her breathing became hoarse and rapid – her heavy shoulders shook and her temples glistened. Then, with a strange squawking shriek, she began to hurl herself into the most spectacular convulsions. It was an amazing, miraculous discharging of energy. Amelia leaped, ducked, somersaulted, swivelled and soared through the air for two hours without a single halt. It was the most wonderful demonstration of physical agility imaginable. 'You must have fed your servant for a year on grasshoppers,' a man joked to father, who responded with a look of gloomy reproof.

When she had finished, the crowd was a quaking body of applause. Amelia stepped forward with a startled grin. The ginger-haired man kissed her hand and handed her a prize of ten gold pieces and a pair of silver buckled pumps. Dyfric pocketed the coins, remarking to Father, 'The Devil must be put to work for the Lord before we may consider banishing him.'

'Holy man,' a voice interrupted. 'I have been looking for you, for I have a complaint.'

Dylfric's eyes stood out a little. 'What are you doing here?' he gasped.

The armless man loomed over him like an ominous pole. He was no longer smiling – indeed his face resembled an onion with a grievance. 'Foot-juggling mainly,' he replied. 'But that is by the by, for I wish to claim my money back. Your bedstraw did not work. All it did was make me sneeze.'

Dylfric pondered this and then asked, 'And what of your bride?'

After a moody, scowling interval, the man bellowed. '*St Elfrida jilted me!*'

A perplexed silence. 'Jilted you!' echoed Dylfric at a loss.

'She ran off with Pogo Nokkes, the one-legged monk of Cannington.'

Dylfric compressed his lips, murmuring, 'You cannot hold me responsible for your misfortune.'

'Before she went,' the man added morosely, 'she gave me this.'

He removed from his jerkin a small silver crucifix. As he held it out, Amelia's eyes bulged and her mouth began to writhe.

The armless man noticed this. 'What is your name, maid?' he enquired.

Her chest began to heave and then her whole body shook.

The armless man smiled. 'She's all aheat,' he exclaimed. 'Trembling with passion.'

Throwing herself forward, Amelia did an amazing aerial somersault followed by a series of cartwheels. I watched her legs gracefully turn over like the spars of a windmill, while Father gritted his teeth and muttered imprecations, for her ebbing skirts had left her stomach and thighs all open to public view once more. She rolled out beyond the stalls to the area of open meadow north of Yardley green. The armless man, admiring her flying legs, cried, 'She is inviting me to give chase!'

Even Dylfric's sparrow-sharp eyes were slits of incredulity. And so were my father's when the fingerless freak, breaking into long prancing strides, began to pursue the revolving skirted figure who had once so faithfully bade us good morning and good night, filled our plates, cleansed our utensils, brought us milk from the dairy, flour from the mill.

# ⇜ 3 ⇝

# LORD PRIAPUS

I mpressed by Dylfric's bleak piety, my father urged me towards the priesthood. After my mother had passed away, there being no tempering influence, I picked up his religious inclinations, attending services at Glastonbury Abbey, reading tales of the Celtic saints and leaving thanks-offerings at local monasteries and hospices.

I do not think I truly had the calling, but perhaps the shock of mother's death had loosened my imagination. At night I found myself projected among regions of saints and angels. The saints were ranting and pale-cheeked like angry ghosts, while the angels had fierce eyes and bore shields like towers of glass. Astride cloud-borne steeds, they pitted their weaponry against demons with elves' eyes and goatish locks who trampled and dunged on pages of the Holy Book. Weird, unhealthy fancies, I see now, arising from the confusions of a child entering manhood, trying to plot a course through a divided and doctrine-pitted world.

If the images of religion were often wild and confusing, its basic precepts seemed temperate and fair-minded, and I was unable to see any clear alternative to the life of prayer and penitence. So therefore, on reaching the age of eighteen, it was arranged that I should train as a novice at a monastery that lay south of the Blackmore Hills.

'Goodbye, my boy,' said Father, embracing me. 'Remember you have chosen rightly. At first, I wished that you might take up a more manly career. But now I know that there are struggles that need not be expressed in broken bones and bloody skulls. Yes, there's bravery in spurning the trappings of temporal valour and withering into that deeper truth that endures when action's at its last gasp.'

'If you say so, Father,' said I, unsure of what he actually meant. 'Did you get the maid to pack plenty of apples and honeycakes in my bag?'

He smiled. 'Yes, you have sweetmeats enough to last you a week.'

I set out from Dykesyat at dawn taking the causeway track running south to Illchester. After two days riding, I stopped by a spring which lay near a ring of trees. The land sloped away steeply to a valley. For camping, I normally choose a level plot, but on that occasion I was feeling tired and not disposed to search around. Erecting a bivouac of cross-sticks, I lined it with ferns and bracken, then lit a fire and cooked myself a broth, adding plenty of seeds, beans and breadcrumbs.

A philosophic mood was taking hold. The quiet star-filled sky, the scent of woodsmoke, a good solid meal – all helped create this feeling of robust satisfaction.

Also, I was eager to become a monk. The previous night my dreams had been embroidered with purple and white vestments, sweet-smelling censers and vellum manuscripts, illustrated with bestiaries and scrollwork. Yes, I was all at one with my choice of career. The priesthood seemed ardent, fastidious, a close brotherhood devoted to the higher mysteries. By comparison, ordinary men seemed crude like those coupling beasts whose behaviour left me in a state of shameful fascination.

The fire was still fervently burning, and I did not want to quench it. The flames made me think of poppies and oranges. After memorising the martyrology and lauds, I said my prayers and prepared to retire to my bivouac, when I heard snorts of laughter followed by rustles coming from the undergrowth. Suspecting robbers, I peered into the shadows, calling, 'Come out and show yourself!'

I was all agog at what happened next. A tall, handsome girl, with tawny-gold hair lapping over her shoulders, stalked out of a dip in the turf beyond the bushes. She walked over, proud and confident as a huntress, which struck me as unusual, for she was entirely naked.

When she came up close, I found myself minutely studying her body. You see, I was brought up in Dykesyat. There I spoke with few women other than serving maids. In order to see one without clothes, I had to walk five miles to Cucklington church where there was a carving of a mermaid. By studying that as a boy, I learned about the top half of a woman and the bottom half of a fish. Hence my notion of how the parts joined up was skew-whiff until the time came when Amelia, taken crazy, showed what had been missing all the while.

Therefore I knew little of matters that really matter, so to speak, when one comes of age. And this girl's body drew me as a moth is drawn to a slender taper of radiance and warmth. White as the campion flower, it was both substantial and graceful and made ruddier and more tempting by the reflected firelight dancing on it, deepening and highlighting the clefts and curves.

The sight of her stirred me at a most profound level. For everything about her was a revelation, from her forehead and shoulders down to the defiant tilt of her breasts and the warm pallor of her thighs.

'What are you laughing at?' I asked when I had recovered.

'Does laughter need a reason?' she replied sharply. 'Must we all know, be able to render in speech, why we feel, how we act?'

'No,' said I. 'I will rest content with mystery for the while.'

'Good. You are beginning to learn.' Her eyes picked me over. 'I saw you muttering to yourself like someone who has lost his wits.'

'I was praying.'

'Praying – to whom?' The girl knelt beside the fire and warmed her palms. 'Tonight is a time of laughter and celebration.'

'Is that why you are not wearing clothes?'

The girl tossed the question aside with a sharp laugh. 'Clothes are like leaves. They are for shedding at the right time and place.'

'That is alright then,' said I relieved. 'I thought you may have been too poor to afford them.'

The barb struck a tender point. 'It is you, not I, who are ridiculous,' she hissed. 'You are a poltroon. Why, look at you, you are wearing everything except your horse's blanket.'

I cast off my brown worsted riding-mittens, saying, 'There, I have made a concession.'

'I should think so. Summer is stirring all around.' She bent over the flames and intoned. 'Tonight we pay honour to Lord Priapus.'

'Who is Lord Priapus?'

'He is the power,' she replied, 'that drives the sap through the branching elm. He is the force that sets the moon in labour. He is fire and lightning and rain striking the dry earth. He is the grunting sow and the rearing stallion. He is the dragon and the dove, the beginning and the end, the cry of the child, the death gasp of the crone. He is the time-defying beast that arises in the night, the Green Man who brandishes the mighty oak tree as his club.'

'Indeed,' said I. 'He sounds a man of versatility.'

The girl smiled and edged closer to me. 'I can show you where he dwells.'

At that moment I was beginning to understand where, for I was acutely conscious of a tickling throb just below my groin. But I was destined for the monastery. If I was to excell in that profession, I must develop the virtues of continence, cleanliness and piety.

'I do not think that I and Lord Priapus and will prove compatible,' I told the girl. 'You see, I am shortly to become a monk.'

'That is all right,' replied the girl. 'Around these parts the priests pay homage to Lord Priapus. This year Father Tumpkin is presiding over the festivities. All the girls will march ahead, crowned with flowers and bearing wands of willows. Father Tumkin will lead the procession, and he will be carrying a big pole. Do you know what will be placed at the top?'

'What?' I was by now most curious.

Her eyes lowered to that unruly part of me. Thinking that she was mocking my pious demeanour, I decided to make a valiant stand. I recalled the vigils of St Anthony and Simeon Stylites and cried, 'Off with you, woman! I am not one for trivial distractions. You seek out the Devil in me. But I have cast the Worm out, as did God Himself, and never will temptation darken my heart. My spiritual instructor, Father Bleatforth, warned me that the flesh is the province of corruption. I know full well the story of David and Abishag – how the brave and noble king debased himself for a few naughty hours. Well, Kings may fall, angels tumble out of heaven, empires wane, but ne'er shall I be brought down. So go woman – go indulge yourself with the swineherds!'

My anger was all mummery and shadow-play. I knew it even then. Still I was intensely proud of my performance and expected the girl to respond with admiration. But instead she quietly stood up and walked away.

'If you are no respecter of Lord Priapus,' she gave a backward glance, 'why do you set up camp here?'

I felt a forlorn lurching in my stomach, and then, paradoxically, I wanted to follow her. When such passions take grip, I realised, one's emotions shift and waver with every passing minute. But I desisted. Her parting-shot left me perplexed, however, and I looked once more at the surrounding terrain. Apart from its steepness, I saw nothing unusual in the site I had chosen.

GALAHAD

A new day dawned flushing the sky pink. Later the first yellow rays silvered the grass. Crawling out of my bivouac, I assessed the situation. I was amazed by the sight that greeted me. For I was standing in the middle of a turf-drawing or carving in the chalk. Trenched in bold white lines was the figure of an enormous naked man, with an upraised club, stepping slightly over to the right.

But I myself was camped on the most noticeable feature. A vastly magnified depiction of that part of me which was becoming increasingly agitated.

As I wandered around the figure, I heard a noise of pounding drums and singing voices. Far below, I saw a troop of people marching up towards me. They were led by a group of maids crowned with garlands of flowers. As they tramped along, they threw off their skirts and shifts, scattering them on the turf and throwing out their arms as if embracing the air. Behind them was a group of four men, wearing skull-caps of stags' horns and beating silver-studded drums decorated with tassells of horsehair.

The maids, by now entirely naked, were rolling in the grass, cupping the May dew in their hands and anointing their skin with its freshness. I knew of the custom from Dylfric who, with strenuous revulsion, had told me how the women of these parts believed the first dew of the month to hold a substance that would ensure perpetual youth and beauty. 'An impious, vain falsehood!' he declared. 'Why, I tried it for myself many times – do I look beautiful or youthful, Galahad?' I agreed that neither quality shone forth from him, and I sensed the swiftness of my assurance stung him a little.

But the maids presently tumbling amid the droplets were in little danger of losing their vitality. As their bodies tangled together, their glazed, shining hindparts stuck out like puffballs. They pulled at each other's legs and slapped each other flanks as though the sound itself was funny. Having got up on their feet, they adjusted their hair and garlands and looked back to see coming up the rear a man in a black-and-scarlet cape carrying a long pole. On the top dangled a representation of that accursed organ which it was impossible to forget around these parts.

The procession tramped over the feet of the naked man and up towards the navel on which I was standing. The maid up front was the same who had introduced herself to me last night. She came bounding towards me, her bare legs gleaming as she strode, her healthy breasts swaying in the clear light.

When she reached me, she stopped and held out something in her hand. It was a plain stick of charcoal. Then she did a most curious thing. Kneeling within a yard of me, she began to draw signs on her naked skin, moons, sunwheels and snaky esses. I stood still, breathing in her swooning closeness, feeling my stunned heart fuse like a stone in the wall of my body. Slowly rising, she stepped towards me and marked my forehead with a sign.

'Stand still!' she ordered as she sketched on my brow. 'The lion must be perfectly formed.'

Finishing drawing, she blew away a few loose specks. Then, throwing down the charcoal, she looped her arms around my neck and scrutinised my face. Her eyes were light-green like the turf. 'I am going to awaken the god in you,' she murmured.

With gentle force, she embraced me. I felt this sense of inevitability – of absolute surrender to the needs of the moment. She pushed her face into mine, closing my

21

mouth with a kiss, and I sank back onto the grass. The next moment I was covered by her live and shining weight. She spread over me like a breathing blanket, making stifling no longer unpleasant. Her legs were strong as stakes as she matched her body to mine. Quickly her fingers undid and removed whatever stuff I was wearing.

I felt an insane jellyfish pleasure. I was all passivity and acquiesence. Verily I was nothing, no head, no reason, no conscience – my intellect was void. Locked in a realm of autonomous delight, cocooned in a calyx of pure sensation – all sounds and scents withdrew. I did not hear the clashing drums. Nor see the band of maids move around us in a garland of linked arms. Nor smell the flowers they pelted on us as we broke and formed in the grass.

Some time later, I stood up and stared down at my body. It was smeared with grass stains and brown earth was engrained in my knee-caps. My tawny-haired companion-in-lust got to her feet and slapped herself until she was pink and tingling. A rush of applause broke into pieces around us. Turning, I saw the group of naked maids who were standing around, blackening their bodies with charcoal and casting glances in our direction. It was as if what they had seen had stoked their desire for participation. A figure stepped out of their midst and they made way for him.

The man in the scarlet and black cape, holding his pole, advanced towards us. Not wanting his standard to quiver, every so often he would cast a fierce glance at it, as if seeking to instil decorum.

'Brother Galahad,' he greeted, 'welcome to our order. I thought you were a novice. But your mastery of religious ritual is a joy to behold. Save for one small point – your *modus operandi* is a little urgent. In future, take things slower – exchange a garland or love-knot perhaps before pushing on to the consecration. It *is* important that we keep up a high standard at all times.'

My hands flew up and hid my face. Such wicked irony had cut me to the quick. I felt gnawed by shame and remorse. I had betrayed my deep religious principles. I was not a man but a creature of the earth, a grunting, truffling beast who took his pleasures wherever they lay.

'I must get to the monastery,' I stammered. 'I have to see the abbot.'

'My name is Father Tumpkin,' the man replied. 'I am the abbot of Cerne Abbas and am officiating at the Maytime festivities.'

Like one who had asked for a glass of water and been given a bucket of brimstone, I stood quivering with disbelief.

'But I thought you worshipped God.'

'Indeed, I do,' said Father Tumpkin. He gestured to the massive carved figure. 'And you are standing on him right now.'

# 4

# THE SIEGE PERILOUS

*Marvelling as to what this could mean, the nobles questioned Merlin,*
*who told them that the seat was reserved for a knight who was absolutely pure,*
*so that did any other adventure himself upon it, he would be straightway*
*swallowed up by the yawning earth.*

After my abortive attempt to become a monk, I considered pursuing law and scholarship, neither of which had appeal for an able-bodied youth. But the knighthood had glamour. It combined brawn and bravado with finesse and discipline. Disregarding Father's advice (after the debacle at Cerne Abbas he wanted me to study law so that all monastic communities in Britain should be prevailed upon to perform the proper Christain rituals) I taught myself the arts of fencing and horse-riding.

My early experience in the martial arts was gained when I took the position of squire to a certain Cambrian knight, Sir Porius Vrontigern. After I had spent three years in his service, he bid me accompany him on a long journey into the western territory, where we saw evidence of the incursions of the Atrebates. This unruly tribe had ridden across the central plain showing neither respect for property or virginity. The only thing they did respect was a circle of enormous stones scattered beyond the Roman town of Sarum. Every morning they would gather within this rude temple and listen to the words of their high priest. Tall, bearded and blue-robed, he held up a star-crowned wand and intoned a prayer before the the altar-block.

'O Belinus, Lord of the Brazen Star, let thy light spill blessing on this tribe. Let the swine and cattle flourish. Let the feather-crested corn grow tall and slender. Let thy dart of stinging gold plump the hazel nut and apple. Protect us with thy self-renewing flame throughout the hanged and ash-cold season until harvest-time, when the earth yields its plenty, so that our babes shall grow up swift-footed, clear-eyed and noble of heart.'

Then, turning to the tribe, he would let out a war-cry, ice-cold as demon's spittle, at which signal they would sweep down the hill and ravage and rape non-stop until sundown.

Sir Porius Vrontigern surveyed the tumbled huts and abandoned bodies. We had ridden far beyond the well-grazed plains and everywhere saw evidence of pillage. The breeze was corrupted by the ebony tang of burning and stray animals wandered around a waste of broken pots and empty compounds.

To avoid a waft of hot blown ash, Sir Porius raised his shield. 'Fire is the most terrible and most loving of elements, Galahad,' he declared when it had passed. 'If you keep it small and contain it with stones, it will warm your hearth, bake your bread and boil your stews. But once you cast it among straw and rushes, leave it to its own devices, its rampant nature surges up and it becomes a tiger of appetite, devouring everything that is dry, sheltering or useful.'

'Like a mighty conqueror whose ravenous pride and ambition will stop at nothing.'

'Exactly.'

I had grown to like Sir Porius's grave, hesitant wisdom, but knew the fight was leaving him. He was becoming like my father. Theology had started plucking at his conscience. The more his mind sprouted doctrines and comparisons, the more his body forfeited that animal energy necessary to besiege and protect walls and fortresses.

'Galahad,' he said, 'you must ride to Camelot – tell King Arthur of these depredations. The time is right, for all the knights will be gathered at Camelot for the Whitsuntide Feast.'

'At your command, sir,' I replied.

I wheeled Larkspur round and began my journey to the south, passsing the high camp of Dolebury, the hamlets of Montacute and Sutton where I rested. Setting forth after a cold night, I climbed to a clump of beeches and, as I descended, the fortress rose up like a fallen fragment of heaven – a dizzying vision of buttressed battlements, lookout towers and gate-houses at the four points of the compass. Slowing Larkspur to walking-pace, I went up to the guard-house, called out my name and business and was let through. Wiping the dust from eyes, I dismounted.

Amid the din of fiddles, strings and tambourines, I entered the feasting-hall where all the knights and dignitaries had assembled. My anxious eyes drank in the colours of the high and raftered hall bedecked with banners and tapestries. Gryphons and crested unicorns disported themselves on the shields mounted on the walls.

At the far end the gold-red dragon of Uther writhed against a woad-blue background. Beneath was Arthur's Round Table, a mighty circle of planed and painted wood mounted on a dais. The King was lofty and massive-shouldered and possessed a grace of sorts. With his proud, mobile countenance and leonine crop of hair, which he wore tumbled and uncombed, every inch he looked the leader. His intent eyes stared straight as an arrow. However, if you kept your glance fixed long enough, they'd lose that piercing brightness and become dim, questioning and lost, like those of a fool and a fantast, and there and then I divined his traits – decisiveness inmixed with dreaming and dawdling. Beside him sat Queen Guinevere, a glowing, apple-cheeked beauty, with a soft ivory bosom and a smile like a merry little candle, and beside her Lancelot, with dark blue eyes and a blunt crag of a nose.

But none of them seemed to witness my entry. I became angry and cursed aloud. Sodding Oddbods! After all, had I not ridden a great distance? Was not my message of great importance? But they did not so much as announce my name. When drink flies down the gullet, thought I, chivalry and manners fly out of window. But I had to try, for Sir Porius considered the Atrebates a terrible threat to the stability of the kingdom.

'My noble Lord Arthur!' I called, mounting the dais in the middle of the hall.

But Arthur did not hear. First he was absorbed by the sight of a champion acrobat. Arrayed in daffodil yellow and spring green, silver bells stitched to his toes and cuffs, he jingled and leapt in the space between the dais and side-tables occupied by the lesser knights.

I called to Arthur twice more. Still he did not hear. Now he had begun to pluck at the laces of a serving girl's bodice. His expression was transfixed, studious, as though opening one of those small pouches containing saints' relics. Meanwhile

Lancelot was reciting to Guinevere a fragment of French poetry, every so often his eyes drooping low and slumbrous as they grazed on the silken pastures of her bosom. Why is it, I thought, that the highest of men are transfixed by the sight of a woman's chest? Here I will slip in a cautionary tale, for it is said of the blessed martyr, St Donyatt of Clobbingwell, that he did cover his eyes with mud whenever he walked around the fair town of Trillington Knockwell lest he come across any of the street women naughtily exposing their bobbies. That way, not knowing where he was, he wandered into a church and the mud slipped away from his eyes. For he saw a most beautiful lady who had on a low-cut dress and was kneeling up by the altar. Straightway did he arraign her for baring so much to the eye, and Lo! he was stuck dumb. For the maid did turn on him – she was none other than the Blessed Virgin herself! So that he should pay for his impudence, that instant St Donyatt sprouted bobbies himself and from thence he was never known to wash or bare his skin to the world!

Clearly exemplars like these had not humbled Arthur. For before the eyes of all his noble knights, he carried on fingering the bodice of the servant girl whose gaze was fixed downwards – she was as interested as he in what his enquiries would disclose. But then Arthur stopped plucking at the laces, the girl breathed out gratefully, and I realised that the noble king was merely aiding a lady whose fittings clasped around her too tightly! Lancelot continued reciting to Guinevere. And the knights went on eating – all eyes and mouths in the grip of that pact that exists between the laden plate and the clamouring stomach. Even if the Atrebates were to march in, throwing flaming brands and spears at them, those knights would continue to barter guffaws and spade smiling blocks of pork into their open hatches.

I shall be bold, I thought, and try to join the knights sitting at the Round Table. I went up and looked around and found, to my surprise, a single chair that was empty – a big, imposing chair with carved, gold-painted eagle's wings as a backrest. It was probably meant for someone haughty and proud, but I deserved it. So I pulled it away, smiled at the knights – who threw up their hands with shock – and sat down. The table went silent, and the knights stared at me with wordless wonder, their mouths making sounds that they could not quite shape into meaning.

Then my ears were pierced by a lean and shattering blast. Two trumpeters were standing at my side, heraldic banners hanging from the long silver stems, and blowing for all their lungs were worth. A gust of silence wafted across the hall; all the murmurings, the scrapings of plates, abruptly ceased. A hundred knights' heads turned and gasped. And now every single member of the banquet, from the King to the serving girls, was staring at me with dilated eyes.

'My Lord Arthur,' said I, rising on my feet. 'I bring a message from the Cambrian knight, Sir Porius Vrontigern. He wishes to inform you of the Atrebates. They have been pillaging and burning…'

The words tripped out, hurried and nervous, and then dried up. Arthur was not listening. Only showing amazement at my whole appearance. I glanced down to check whether there was a hole in my chainmail. But all the links were intact. Yet still he gaped at me, as though I were an apparition.

'My Lord Arthur,' I enquired. 'Is anything wrong. Why do you gaze at me so?'

'Repeat that miracle,' he said.

'What miracle?' said I.

Arthur shivered. He stretched out his hand, forefinger pointing to a place at my back. 'You have sat down on that chair.'

This was indeed a memorable moment. All my life I had valued and prized the reputation of Arthur's court. I had dreamed of meeting and speaking to these knights, whose names I cherished as demi-gods, and now here they all were, regarding me with awe and admiration, and for merely sitting on a chair!

'You have sat down on the Siege Perilous,' Arthur said.

'It does not look so perilous to me,' said I, giving the chair a solid kick. 'The seat is most excellently planed for my buttocks.'

A long silence. All the knights at the banqueting tables kept their gazes fixed – eyes drawing me in like glinting hooks. Some were corpulent and bearded, some clean-shaven, ascetic, like priests, and others were delicate, girl-like novices, looking as though they could not tell a sword-hilt from a blade.

No sound. Only the slurp of dogs' tongues against stone plates. Swish of bustling scullery maids at work beyond the main hall. Then Lancelot broke the peace. Standing, he threw out his arms, clapped his sides and let out the heartiest laugh I have ever heard.

'What is your name, sir?' he asked.

'Galahad,' said I.

Lancelot looked across to Arthur and Guinevere. It was a confident stare, implying his authority or favouritism held weight. 'I like this Galahad. He has a sturdy wit.' He mimicked my tone but somehow made it seem fluting, effete. 'The seat is most excellently planed for my buttocks.'

The hall quaked with laughter. I thought the walls would shake themselves flat like the ones at Jericho. Everyone rolled around and roared. They clashed plates with knives, thumped the tables, stamped and clapped, their moist and wine-flushed faces grinning at me with an enthusiasm that I found inexplicable.

I reflected on what a curious age it was. Spells and supersitions, deserving of mockery, were treated with gravity, while a tranquil comment on a chair was rated as a pinnacle of wit. But who was I to complain? If the reason was inscrutable, I had at least made my mark. This was evident when Arthur smiled and gestured me to join him at the Round Table.

Sinking comfortably into the Siege Perilous, I enjoyed a solid fare: venison, eggs, beans, samphire, mashed turnips, garlic and butter sauce washed down with malty ale and apple wine. But my enjoyment of the food was spoilt by the excessive amazement which everyone around me was expressing.

'Look,' said I, 'you have here in this hall professional acrobats and musicians, jugglers, tumblers and fiddlers, and they have all mastered the art of sitting down, as you have yourselves, and so I honestly see no reason for this attention.'

But that only made them laugh all the more.

# 5

# THE CHURL

S ir Hugh Meadmore swung his horse round. 'Look at that vile crone standing by the tree!' he exclaimed pointing. I sighed. After serving five years at Arthur's court, five years of keeping down the Atrebates, rescuing men and maidens, practising group charges, tilting and jousting, I had become weary of being a knight errant, weary of my vows of poverty, obedience and chastity, and weary of men like Sir Hugh Meadmore, who were incapable of sorting out fact from fable.

It was not entirely his fault, for there are by-ways of fate and disposition that place all kinds of follies at our door. Meadmore had come of a high-born, rich family, but he had forfeited his father's love by laxity of habit and excessive indulgence in wine. To make amends, he opted to become a knight and, in the first year at Camelot, had shown vigour and resolve, attending chapel and assisting in various raids and rescues. But of late the cider orchards of Avalon had drawn him into their bowery bosom and weakened and bloated his spirit. And now, instead of riding forth and seeking noble deeds, he spent his time dimly riding round in circles or reclining under a tree drinking pitcher after pitcher of the wretched juice while reciting local rhymes of lustihood and debauchery. In his sober moments, he would express shame at his ways but would later relapse. Unremitting indulgence had started to interfere with his vision. He was forever describing things in a way that bore no relation to their texture or semblance.

'She is skinny and wizened with warts all over her face,' he went on. 'Her nose is all crooked, like a bent dagger, and her mouth is nothing but a gaping slit. Her snaky grey hair is like the Gorgon's locks, and she has one huge red eye in the middle of her forehead.'

I glanced across to the woman and replied.

'Meadmore, you drink excessively and see things all wrong. The woman by the tree is a fair maid with well-shaped breasts and a slender figure. She has fine silky hair, yellow as the gorse, and an extremely pretty mouth. That huge red eye you see is a is a rare and costly ruby that is attached to a headband.'

He blinked. 'I do not know what you are talking about.'

'I am talking about you, Meadmore,' I told him. 'What is wrong with you? You seem to have this obsession about vile crones. You see ugliness in women where there is only beauty.'

Our discourse was interrupted by the fair maid. Leaving the tree, she ran over to us and knelt down sobbing. She flung out her arms in despair. I eased Larkspur to a halt.

'A boon, a boon, Sir Galahad!' she cried.

'What would you have of me?' I asked, taken aback by her distress.

'I cry for vengeance on a churlish knight, who has separated my love from me.'

'Tell me your story and make it quick,' said I.

'I was betrothed to a gallant knight,' she began. 'And we were entirely happy until yesterday. We were riding out together, planning our marriage, and we came over the moorland to Tarn Witherpool, where there stood a huge castle on a crag, with streamers flying and banners waving in the wind. As my love and I looked up at the mighty keep, a horrible and churlish warrior, twice the size of a mortal man, rushed forth in complete armour. Grim and fierce-looking, he was armed with a huge club, and he bade my knight to leave me to him and go hence. Whereupon my love drew his sword to defend me, but the giant brought down his club with terrible force, knocking the sword from his hand. Then, seizing him, the churlish knight caused him to be flung in a dungeon. He then returned and sorely treated me, saying that, if I would go to Arthur's court, I may find a champion to avenge me. I beg of you, Sir Galahad, noblest and bravest of all the knights, to defend the honour of my love and help us be reunited.'

I felt sorely angered hearing this. Sir Hugh Meadmore, however, did not seem to have taken in any of the fair maid's tale. Instead he was staring at her, screwing up his eyes, blinking and rubbing them, as though still unresolved as to what exactly he was looking at.

Thank God my response was firm and positive. 'I vow by my knighthood,' I told her, 'that I will ride forth and find that proud giant and will not rest until I have overpowered him.'

'Oh Sir Galahad!' cried the maid, seizing my hand and kissing it. 'What can I do to show my gratitude.'

'We will defer the consideration of pleasurable dalliance,' said I. 'Meantime I will do your bidding.'

Leaving Meadmore perplexed, I galloped north over the wild lands. It was a lonely, arduous journey to Tarn Witherpool, over miles of marsh and bracken, and I felt relieved when I saw the small bright lake gleaming amid a basin of low green hills.

Before me towered the giant's castle, black and gold banners flaunting themselves defiantly in the wind.

I drew my sword and sounded my horn.

'Come forth, proud knight!,' I called. 'Sir Galahad is here to punish you for your misdeeds. If you are afraid, come forth and yield yourself my thrall.'

The gates of the drawbridge creaked upwards. Out charged a gigantic oaf, over seven feet tall and waving an enormous club. I was amazed at his slovenliness. His armour was all rusted and unoiled; many of the plate-links were rattling and hanging loose and his hauberk was falling apart. He was pot-bellied, yellow-toothed, with arms and thighs that could have flattened a stone wall. There was little doubt as to his health and agility. He was driving down towards me like a bull on heat, with his knobbed club held aloft like a small tree. Being on horseback, I eased Larkspur over slightly. The hulking brute charged past me borne along by his own impulsion.

'Have you no horse?' I enquired. 'You cannot fight on legs alone. I could just gallop round you all morning.'

'That may be true,' the churl sneered. He walked back towards me and spat contemptuously in the grass. 'But still you are unable to release the knight betrothed to the maid. He is locked up in my dungeon and, if you as much as touch me with your sword, I will give him a good pummelling with my club.'

'Heavens!' I exclaimed. 'Where is your chivalry, man?'

'Listen,' said the churl. 'I'll strike a bargain. You must swear solemnly, by the Holy Rood, that you will return here at the same hour next week and bring me the true answer to a certain question. If you are able to do that, I will release the knight. If not, you too must become my prisoner and hand over all your lands to me.'

'I have no property,' I told him.

'Do you accept my terms?' he said.

I shrugged. No logic – a typical Dark Age mentality.

'Alright,' I said after a while. 'What is this question?'

The churl grinned. 'My question is simply this. What is it that all women most desire?'

Agreeing to his terms, I swore by the Holy Rood, then galloped back to Camelot. What a question! Surely different women want different things. First I put the question to Sir Lancelot. He produced a slow, complacent smile and patted his pelvic girdle. 'Is Lancelot a loon?' I ask myself. It is not as if every hen-keeper, doorman and beggar, rabbit, flea and ant does not have one. Listen, I want this not whispered around, but I think it is because Lancelot comes from Gaul, and I have it, on good report, that in Gaul ladies who will allow you a 'boon' should you offer them total devotion in the period from Michaelmas to Christmas. However, come Christmas, once they've gotten their gifts, they start to look around for another. Now, there you have it, the solemn facts of the matter.

Still the question was: What is it that all women most desire? And being less than content with Lancelot's reply, I contacted the other knights and posed the same riddle. They retorted in many different ways. I made a quick list:

Love
Happiness
Health
Money
Gold torques encrusted with emeralds
Swan-feathered beds
Squirrel-furred snoods with matching jackets
Ratskin riding gloves embroidered with seed-pearl
A duckfeather hat
Handsome husbands with small tight buttocks and enormous estates.

But none of these answers seemed right. They were either too small and strict or too broad and wallowing. As a last resort, I decided to visit Merlin, who then resided in a limestone grotto in the Great Forest of Mendip. The setting was fittingly shady and mysterious for a purveyor of practical occultism. A stream issued out of the base of a shaggy-browed cliff. Half-way up was the mouth of a cavern from which descended a flight of rock-cut steps. This was the entrance to the wizard's residence. Impetuously I dashed up the steps and hurried through the first chamber.

'Wait there, will you?' called a harsh voice.

I drew back abruptly. Merlin was seated on the latrine bent over a text on demonology.

Grimly I faced the wall, until I heard a long sigh followed by the rustle of animal skin being hoisted in place. I turned and addressed the magician who was securing his belt.

'Merlin, I wonder if you could help me.'

'Wait!' he said. 'I have not yet fed the salamanders.'

He went over to a small furnace in the corner. Scooping up some red hot cinders, he spaded them into an iron cage dangling from the ceiling. Inside were two red-scaled lizards of repellent aspect who eagerly gobbled their mineral curry and rasped their appreciation. 'I call them Jasper and Ruby,' he explained. 'Splendid pets for a cold winter – their bodies retain heat indefinitely. I often warm my feet on them.'

'Merlin,' said I, 'I have a question that is sorely vexing me.'

His dark heavy-lidded eyes turned towards me. There was no sparkle in them. It was as if they were weary with all-knowing and desired to linger upon some uncomplicated pastoral scene.

'What is it then?' he said testily. 'I tire of vultures pecking my brain.'

'Merlin, I wish to know: what is it that all women most desire?'

Frowning, he cast down the trowel and drew in his long silver cloak, as if he felt a sudden chill. He swayed a little, visited by a sudden dizziness, then made a great play of searching for his lens. Eventually he found a slate box beneath the cave-floor from which he removed a tiny glinting object. Clenching the glass disc, he reached for a massive tome which lay beside a crystal ball and picked it up. 'Here,' he said opening it, 'I can tell you the five and fifty names of Beelzebub.'

I shook my head.

Turning he asked with exaggerated friendliness, 'How would like a list of the dimensions of the most ancient and sacred Temple of Solomon?'

'I am not seeking occult knowledge, Merlin. Come on, man. You must have an inkling of the answer.'

'Listen to this!' He feverishly fingered the pages. 'I have here a spell which will enable you to make insects appear. Yes, ants, centipedes, caterpillars, spiders – out of thin air. Silkworms too – they'll spin precious garments at your bidding. You will be able to wear a brocaded cape, like those bartered by the merchants of Toulouse. You will be able to command the ants to build you a miniature palace.'

'Merlin, that is not my wish.' Again I repeated the question.

His hands fled to his brow and he began to knead his temples. I waited patiently while he did this. Then, to my disgust and horror, he began to drip black sweat. It was awful to behold. Demons were quarrelling in his head. The book dropped from his hands.

'What is wrong Merlin?'

'Ask me,' he groaned mournfully, 'how to gauge the brightness of a butterfly's wing. Ask me the name of the waterfall where the white hart swims at noon. Ask me whether a young bullock will ever grow wings and fly. Ask me why the blood flows quicker at full moon. Ask me why snowflakes are patterned like chased silver. Ask my why the oyster is sacred to Aphrodite. Ask me what are the numbers and correspondences that make the magic square of Mars. Ask me the texture, weight, consistency of the hind leg of a fly. Ask me how to make talismans, trinkets, spells and amulets. Ask me how to cure warts, ague, chillblains, leprosy, flu and falling sickness.'

I was by now highly irritated. 'Merlin,' I almost shouted. 'What is it that women most desire?'

He gave a loud groan and crashed to the ground. I felt sorry for the shattered hulk lying there pathetically mumbling, 'Wert that I knew, wert that I knew…'

With the question posed by the churlish knight still unsolved, I rode back north, stopping on the way to tarry with Livia. A comely daughter of a taverner, who liked to follow the adventures of various knights and minstrels, she told me what fellow had taken a liking to this or that lady and who had been unhorsed at tournaments or awarded a garter or kerchief. I learned much about how people dressed. There was one young man in town, I was told, who wore a short tunic, with a knive and baselard hanging at his girdle. A second man had a habit lined with fur or silk. A third had a hood which was the colour of claret. A fourth had a long beard with a ring on his finger. A fifth fellow was very poor and went about smeared in feathers and shitte. A sixth poor wight went about with nought on save a pink ribbon tied to hs ankle – he had gone crazy! Faith, I had had enough! I told her that it was not what a man wore that mattered but what lay underneath.

'And what is underneath you, Galahad?' she asked.

So it came to pass, by such wiles, I was prevailed upon to show something of myself. And Livia in turn removed her gown and inevitably I found myself committing those same errors for which I had criticised Lancelot.

No long after, Livia stared at me as if I had acted all wrong.

'Galahad, do you love me? You tarry here only to do one thing, and when that is over, you put your sword back in your scabbard and sally forth into the world again.'

'I honestly do not know,' said I, 'what women truly want.'

'All women,' replied Livia smiling, 'will have there own way, and that is their chief desire.'

'What did you say then?' gasped I. 'Repeat that.'

'Oh that!' Livia wrinkled her nose. 'I was quoting an old riddle. It was much in favour last year. No one finds it funny now. Why are you shaking, Galahad? What has got into you?'

'Repeat what you said, please Livia.'

'All women,' said Livia, 'will have their own way, and that is their chief desire.'

Knowing this was surely correct, I bade Livia goodbye and set off again. When I reached the castle, the churl was waiting outside the drawbridge. He flourished his club in a most challenging manner.

'Have you found the answer to my question?'

'Yes I have.'

I told him what Livia had taught me. Immediately the giant started to wax furious. 'A curse upon the person who has told you this! It must have been my sister, for none but she knew the answer. I vow to heaven that, if I can catch her, I will kill her most horribly, for she has cheated me out my victory.'

'Listen,' said I. 'It was not your sister who told me, but a lady friend of mine called Livia, and there is nothing secret about this riddle. It has been in circulation among country folk for the past year. Only you, living out here in the wilds, have not been aware of that.'

But the churl seemed unmoved by reason. His eyes bulged like huge blue berries, and he chewed the knob of his club with rage. 'I hate you!' he roared. 'I hate the whole world. I will smite it open with this club. I will beat that knight until he is a mere stain on the dungeon-floor. I will find my sister and tear her arms off. I will set alight to the cornfields and smash up the churches. I will eat sheep and frogs and stick pins in butterflies and mount them on the pages of books. I will tear down the cliffs, eat the moon and blow out the sun.'

'You must not say such things,' said I. 'You will get yourself in trouble with the authorities.'

But my words made no impression. He continued to rave, pace and roar like a demented Jupiter. Then I had an idea. Sliding off my mount, I got down and knelt before him on the grass. Assuming a deadly serious expression, I peered into the dense, troubled wall of his face. Very slowly, emphasising each single word, I asked, 'How many cows' tails does it take to reach to the moon?'

Hearing this, he frowned and began chewing at his club again. I saw immediately that I had over-estimated his capacities. He began to blink and grimace, as though the riddle were causing him deep pain and vexation. His teeth bit harder against the knob of his club, and, as he pondered the problem, he actually tore off strips of oak which he involuntarily chewed to pulp with his large yellow teeth. A stream of saliva trickled from the corner of his mouth. Finally he threw his club away and let out a loud and desolate groan.

I did not want to rouse his frenzy any more. I saw that he was not a truly dangerous fellow, only a rather sad figure who had perhaps been teased as a youth for his lack of intelligence.

'I'll tell you the answer,' I told him. 'Now just sit down quietly and listen. This is a truly secret riddle – my grandmother told it me. Everyone has forgotten it by now, and you can feel you are keeping a real secret this time.'

He sat down on the grass and gazed up with meek, passive eyes. His mouth hung open like a hungry dog's.

'How many cows' tails does it take to reach the moon?' He repeated the question as if pleading.

I paused, allowing the tension to build up a fraction more, then smiling said very quietly. 'Only one if it be long enough.'

No reaction at first. He seemed to be poring over the answer, repeating each word slowly, as if fingering them and examining their textures and weights. About quarter of an hour passed in this manner, and then a flush of comprehension spread from his cheeks outwards. Eventually the bolt penetrated to the core. His mouth dimpled in a grin, and his fingers went to his lips like a child who had been delighted with a very special present. And now his jubilant eyes were glowing like bluebells on a March morning. Initially a few tremors, a trembling of the arms, a shaking of the ribs, and then a great shudder of laughter shook his frame; tears poured down his cheeks and he began to roll over in the grass convulsed with mirth.

I waited around, feeling tolerant towards him yet rather bored. Another quarter of an hour passed before he had sufficiently recovered from the jest to be able to stand on his feet. 'Are you alright now?' said I finally.

He nodded, then asked, 'Have you any others like that?'

'Quite a few,' I replied. 'Only I will not tell you them until you release the knight from the dungeon.'

Straightway he agreed. The knight was released and the two of us were entertained by the churl who provided us with a most delicious banquet, throughout which I was prevailed upon to dredge up the mustiest, dustiest drolleries from the vaults of my memory.

# 6

# GRAIL SEEKER

When I returned from Tarn Witherpool, I delivered the knight to his lady and then presented Livia with a gift for solving the riddle. 'Thank you, Galahad,' she said, holding up a long-sleeved gown I had got for her.

'It is of the best mud-resistant cloth,' said I, 'sturdily stitched, so that it will resist the teeth of pigs and dogs and last more than ten years.'

'But then it will no longer be the latest fashion.'

'My dear Livia, what is fashion but a butterfly!'

And with that, I presented her my second token of appreciation – a tiny gold, enamel brooch, precisely crafted in the shape of a Chalkwell Blue.

'That is so beautiful,' she exclaimed. 'I want to burst into tears.'

'Which brings me to my third present,' I burst in gallantly, 'an exquisitely chased silver weeping-dish which ladies at court use to cry into, after their knights have left them.'

I handed Livia the dish. But she did not take it. Instead a shadow spread over her face – the look of one from whom a myriad of small, twinkling moments had been withdrawn. Finally she did take – no, snatch! – the dish from me, hold it up high and return it with the full force of her forearm. It missed my head and glanced harmlessly off my shoulder.

'Get out, Galahad!' she cried. 'And don't ever return!'

My next duty was to attend the wedding of the knight and the lady. The ceremony was held in a small Norman church of Wolfeton, where the knight's father had a manor, and the celebration in the the wooden feasting-hall that lay beside it. To my surprise, the Churl was among the guests, too – capital marks there, for chivalry and forgiveness! He was all dressed up for the occasion. The top half of his body was clad in what seemed like a huge bird-cage, but which he assured me was the latest fashion in tunics. He was a littled sad, too, complaining he had wanted to be a page boy! I dare not tell him he was too large, bristly and inelegant, but edged away gently, fearing he might still retain that insatiable appetite for childish mirth.

Alas! No time for me to enjoy the feasting. No sooner had I plunged my knife into a slab of venison than a messenger entered the hall and made straight for me.

'Galahad, the King desires to see you.'

I found Arthur in the chapel. He had been musing no doubt on great matters. A soft and ardent glow suffused his eyes. He was clad in a black cloak speckled with golden stars, denoting a mystical mood. I knew that he would prove stubborn and intractable.

'Take a pew, Galahad,' he ordered.

I sat. Arthur rested his elbow on a table-tomb and looked at me gravely. 'Since you have been away, a great change has overcome the court. We have all seen a marvellous thing. The Holy Grail appeared during the Eastertide feast. It hovered above the Round Table, streaming fire and radiance. Some of us were struck blind for days.'

I coughed. 'Sire, are you sure it was the Grail and not some trickery of nature that you witnessed? I have heard that many miracles can be attributed to ball-lightning.'

'No, Galahad,' Arthur said firmly, 'it was truly the Grail. As it hovered in a cloud of glory, I heard an angelic choir and felt the spirit stir in me again. I recognised we had become lax at Camelot, tardy of spirit and neglectful. The Grail was there to revive us, to urge us on to holier, nobler things.'

'If you feel religion coming on,' said I, 'how about a jaunt to Glastonbury Abbey? On the Pilgrim's Way there is many a lusty tavern.'

Arthur clasped his forehead and released a long sigh. He replied with a measure of impatience. 'I am talking of a most high and noble aspiration, Galahad, not a pretext for drunken debauchery. You have only lately returned from the wilds. Perhaps you are unaware that over half my knights are gone. Questing for the Grail. I have ordered them to recover it and bring it back to Camelot.'

'Let us hope that they find it,' said I.

''Tis not possible that they all should find it,' Arthur remarked sagely.

'Unless there be more than one Grail, sire.'

'Do not complicate matters, Galahad,' said Arthur frowning. He mounted the steps leading to the altar, and then turned to me solemnly. 'I wish you to consider this quest.'

'Why me, sire?'

'As a knight, you have special gifts. Only you are able to sit on the Siege Perilous.'

'Frankly, I doubt that, sire,' said I, rebellion stirring in my breast. 'The chair will accept rumps far worthier than mine, but none have ventured upon the seat, fearing the earth might open up and swallow them, which is exceedingly unlikely. My own view is that too much has been made of that whole episode. I am tired of people mentioning it. In fact, the whole matter makes me sick. Sodding Oddbobs, sire! Endless deeds of valour I've done since that accursed day, yet all I get from you – and the other knights – is prattle about sitting on that very ordinary chair. Faith, I've a mind to take an axe to it.'

Arthur rapped a stone pillar. 'Calm yourself, Galahad.'

'I shall not calm myself, sire. You've upset me now.'

I could see that I had pricked Arthur with my discourse, but he maintained a level tone. 'It is only that you deny your abilities, Galahad,' he said. 'You put on the mask of the clown.'

Avoiding his eyes, I breathed out harshly. 'You wish me to go forth and seek the Grail?'

Arthur nodded. 'You have qualities that lift you far above the common run of knights.'

'Sire,' said I, 'you ensnare me in coils of praise. But that is only in the hope that I will rise to the expectations and flatteries you bestow. That, in short, I will risk body and soul to satisfy your needs. Did you know there are times I would rather have been born a snorting swine than a valiant knight? Think sire, no swine is expected to rise above his swinishness. No swine need worry about oaths or fealties. No swine is ordered to desert his home, lay down his life and bring back the Grail.'

'Galahad,' Arthur began to grind his teeth, 'I am sorry that God, by some deficiency of divine foresight, has denied you the pleasures of trough and sty which you so earnestly crave. But that is hardly a matter I can correct. Pray let us return to topics of greater consequence. How stands it with you? Speak frankly. Will you seek out the Grail in the right spirit?'

He had thrown the gauntlet in my face. Did I wish to seek the Grail? To undertake a solemn quest while lacking profound conviction? I did not know. True, I had acquired the habit of obedience, not out any desire for servitude, but from a rooted belief that fate bestows the choicest adventures upon those who pursue a rigid code.

'Well sire,' said I with a shrug, 'if that is your wish, I will be happy to oblige. But are you sure this object is of special value? Or is it merely another whim? Last year you sent us looking for the scales of a certain dragon, which you claimed would rejuvenate you. Before that, sire, you had us all galloping around Palestine searching for the Blessed Virgin's robe, which was supposed to make Guinevere fruitful. And before that, you ordered the knights to find a tooth from the Cornish giant Bolster – to endow you with fabulous strength. We found all these relics in time, sire, and took them back to your court, where they are all piled up somewhere. But you have never been satisfied with them for any length. They lie around, making the place look untidy, their powers unproven or exhausted. Meanwhile your attention wanders to an entirely new sacred bauble. And now it is the Grail.'

Two bright roses of rage spread across Arthur's cheeks. 'You are most insolent, Galahad. Faith, I would have you whipped for your impertinence!'

'I am sorry, sire. It was the way I was raised. My father thought it sinful to interfere with natural expression.'

'You do not wish to go on this mission?'

I shrugged. 'I shall poke around a bit, if you should wish it, sire. But I do not see the value of this Grail, this mere object. What is it supposed to do?'

Arthur drew his robe around him tight. His brow grooved and he glared darkly at me. 'You are a fool, Galahad, a jesting heathen, who makes remarks unworthy of a knight. The Grail is not an object, but an idea, a symbol, a principle. It is the cup of life, the overflowing of spiritual energy. What it is made of – whether embossed with gems or carved of common wood – is of no account. It is what it stands for. Men care little for starry abstractions, which they cannot see or take into their hands. But the Grail unites spirit and substance. You can touch it, drink from it, yet it is all afire – burning with the divine breath of the Holy Spirit.'

I gave a wary nod. His eloquence had once made me feel eager at the prospect of finding Bolster's tooth. Until I actually saw the decayed slab of useless bone.

But instead of voicing further doubts, I replied, 'Sire, your words have moved me. I will look for the chalice.'

Arthur smiled, an eager child again. 'Good for you, Galahad. You have made the right choice.'

'Do you have a notion where I might begin this quest?' I asked. 'Where was the Grail last seen? Is anyone learned in its movements.'

Arthur ran his hands along the altar rail and narrowed his eyes. 'There is an elderly king of the Durotriges, called Cealwin, who claims knowledge of its where-abouts. At the time of the next full moon I suggest you contact him, and where you go from there is up to you.'

'The Durotriges of Maiden Castle?'

'Yes, they revere horses above all other animals.'

'Shall I wear a mane and tail then, sire?'

'Silence, Galahad. Your humour is childish for a knight of your years.'

I looked down at the floor, feigning shame. 'Since my wit is to be endured rather than enjoyed, I shall set off now, sire. And I hope for your sake this wonder-cup, this Holy Grail, will prove worthy of the the time and effort.'

Picking up my helmet, I left the chapel. As I passed under the arched doorway, Arthur called after me. 'Close the lych-gate when you leave, please Galahad. The day before I found a cow grazing upon the chapel tapestries.'

# 7

# KING CEALWIN

I followed Arthur's instructions and waited until the next full moon. Then I made contact with the tribe who, after giving me a baleful welcome, invited me to join in their sunrising ceremony. At twilight I found myself sitting at the edge of a stone circle with a group of dour-looking Durotriges. King Cealwin – could you actually call him that? – looked like an old decaying fish dredged up from a riverbed. Seated solemnly before the altar stone, bull's horns mounted on his head, he waited for the ceremony to begin.

The faces of the Durotriges standing round were painted blue-black with berry juice, so that they resembled a pack of Ethiops, the whites of their eyes prominent. They dawdled on the perimeter of the circle in their coarse blue worsted tunics and leather jerkins. Some of their expressions were most incredibly stupid, reminding me of an old dog I knew; he would gaze fixated at a squirrel on a branch; the rodent would whip out of sight, yet the old hound continued looking with stricken fascination, until I gave him a bone or tickled his ear.

Action at last. A flutter of murmurs whipped through the ranks of lookers-on. A white horse walked into the middle of the circle led by a man about my age, quite good-looking in a coarse sort of way, with thick gold locks, drooping moustache and a band of foxfur around his arm. Loud cheers accompanied his appearance.

But it is the mare which was the more remarkable, a gleaming, silken-flanked beast – a true foal of Epona. She was very agitated and tossed back her neck but the man tried to soothe her by stroking and whispering. The horse responded to his gentleness, ceasing to paw with her hooves, and then he bent down on all fours, saying: 'Rhiannon, you and I are of the same family. What is man but horseflesh? I prostrate myself before you. I desire to become one with you – you who raced while giving birth to twins. I want your strength, speed, power and pride. So I beg your indulgence, mother of many foals, for my humble act of worship.'

The man got to his feet and began to stroke the horse. He rubbed his cheek against its nose, whispering gentle, beseeching words, until the creature relaxed and sank on its knees. The man crouched down next to the horse, head resting against its mane, hand slung round its next, still soothing and coaxing, so that it became oddly quiescent.

Then two elderly men entered. They were carrying a big wood-and-leather trough about the size of a small boat. Setting it down beside the resting mare, they went away and returned holding heavy pottery jars, which they unsealed and poured into the trough. My stomach quivered. The jars were abrim with blood and offal, acquired from the Samain sacrifices and stored for ceremonial occasions. Steam arose from the basking contagion, indicating it had been flame-heated, presumably to enhance its vileness.

How I detested the sight! I had to turn away. The knights at Camelot had described this ceremony in richly ironic tones, vying with each other in exclamations of disgusted superiority. Wanting nothing of it, I cast around for a likely route of exit, but then I heard the old King's voice. 'Grail-seeker,' he intoned, 'I invite you to drink soup with me.'

I did not want to. It was vile. It was pointless. It was utterly degrading. But what could I do? I was supposed to be looking for the Grail, and the King was thought to have knowledge of its whereabouts; therefore my attitude to him had to be placatory.

I turned around with a shudder. The man and the mare were still kneeling beside the blood-filled bath and staring curiously at the King who was shedding his clothes. Naked he entered the blood-bath, sinking himself in comfortably and patting the horse, who was hanging its head warily over the trough. Obviously the creature was accustomed to ceremonial blood-smells – any ordinary horse would be gripped by terror. Sitting upright, King Cealwin extended a scrawny dripping arm, inviting me to come and join him. A constellation of hostile eyes were suddenly nailing me back – eyes that regarded any sense of delicacy as a show of arrogance. I had no choice.

So I strode over to the King, and, still keeping my armour on, climbed in opposite him, immersing myself in the offal and steaming stench. The ancient, wind-scored face regarded me tiredly, arms laid over the sides of the trough. His tongue slipped out like a snail taking exercise and began lapping up the warm stew.

'It is good Grail-seeker,' he said. 'Drink it yourself. You will then have many sons.'

I told him quietly that I had already eaten and tried to shift the conversation to what was uppermost in my mind.

'Where is the chalice?' I asked. 'I hear it has been seen around these parts.'

He frowned, removed one blood-soaked arm and reached over to the mare. Stroking its nose, he gazed into its gentle, bemused eyes and asked. 'Rhiannon, mother of foals, mistress of the seven winds, look into the blood, the scarlet food of life, and tell this knight where is the Grail.'

The mare trembled its nostrils and emitted a loud snort. The King glanced at me and pronounced solemnly. 'Wales.'

Wales, he said, Wales. If I had asked him where the tide had gone, or where the birds had migrated, he would have said Wales. That was his stock answer to any question demanding a specific location. He was old and his brain was going and one could not expect much better from a Durotrige. Wales. It must simplify life considerably, I thought, when one has a vocabulary of only a few words. I thought the Romans introduced the rudiments of education in this land. One can only presume that they took it back when they left!

I asked, 'How did the horse acquire the information?'

He did not reply. Instead he began humming to himself, blocking off my enquiries. It was all nonsense, of course. What was Arthur doing? Musing in his chapel, among painted glass and Spanish tiles, imagining a golden chalice trailing clouds of glory, while I was up to my neck in blood broth and consulting a dumb animal as an authority.

A commotion among the Durotriges. They began shouting and shaking their spears. King Cealwin stirred the purple liquid with his feet. Anxiously he looked across to the tribe, who were breaking apart and making room for a knight on horseback. Into their midst he rode astride a pure black horse draped all over with green silk. I recognised the golden falcon on the black shield as that of Sir Bors, a former knight of Camelot. Trotting up to the bath, he looked down on King Cealwin and I.

'Galahad!' he cried. 'What are you doing up to your neck in animal blood in a bath with a filthy old man?'

'If you must know, I am looking for the Holy Grail.'

'Faith, have you dropped it in the tub?'

'No, I am asking King Cealwin for information, and I am sharing the bath with him purely as a ritualistic nicety.'

Sir Bors wrinkled up his nose. 'Rather you than me.'

'Do not be supercilious, Bors,' said I angrily. 'If you are a knight on a mystical quest, you have to to put truth before personal hygiene.'

Sir Bors raised a dubious eyebrow. 'I still find it all rather unsavoury, Galahad. However, if you yearn for more civilised pleasures, why not rest a few days at my castle, which lies two miles to the east in the valley of the Horning Brook? I'd enjoy hearing the news from Arthur's court, and my young wife, Juliet, will see that you're comfortable.'

# 8

# HERE BE DRAGONS

A ll in all,' said Sir Bors, 'I am satisfied with my life. Yet I do sometimes worry, for the more wordly goods I acquire, the more restless grow my hungers. In fact, since you last visited, Galahad, I have carried out further improvements. Let me show you the angle turrets and strapwork.'

Bors was a good – if complacent – host. After sampling the disgusting bathing habits of King Cealwin, I was grateful for the civilised pleasures afforded by a stay in his castle. I followed him across the courtyard and past the stables to the stone-flagged steps that rose briskly to the battlements. On top the wind was blowing, yet the scene below was pastoral, serene. I looked out across the deer park. There was a stream and a lake and fat cattle grazed in meadows shaded by big chestnuts.

'Imagine,' murmured Bors, 'all this space and beauty is mine.'

'What you mean Bors,' said I, 'is that you have swept the serfs off the common land and built a big wall around the place.'

'Of course, Galahad – all ownership is based upon someone else's dispossession.'

'Is that why you keep at guard at the door – fearing what you take shall be taken back?'

'Galahad, you are acquiring your father's preaching habits. But think on this! Given time, all of us will inherit something that once belonged to another. There will be changes and invasions. Our worldly goods will be churned around like sand in the tide. No single grain stays, and you cannot say whether that's for good or bad, it is simply the way of things. And I am merely reaping a little for myself before someone – or something – snatches it away.'

'True enough, Bors!' said I, taken aback by his stoicism. 'So let us hope the fair weather holds.'

'You have not seen my new chapel, have you?' he asked, urging my appreciation back to his acquisitions. 'A minor triumph in its way. I've found this most skilled builder, a modest man with temperate habits. His pointing and coursing cannot be bettered – I can recommend him to anybody. His services are extremely reasonable. We give him clean water out of a brass dish each day and some free bread and eggs, and he is perfectly happy.'

'I would not work for that,' I told him. 'You may well end up damned if you do not show more consideration for your employees.'

'Actually,' he replied, 'that is not technically possible. You see, I employ a full-time chantry priest to say prayers both for myself, my loved ones and my ancestors, and he is extremely well-paid.'

'Heaven is then guaranteed.'

'Absolutely.'

'All this is very pleasing, Bors,' I told him. 'But I do find it rather tame. There is more to being a knight than fancy brickwork and a priest trilling away like a blackbird to ensure one's sinecure in paradise.'

Sir Bors produced a smooth and padded amile. 'Yes, I have more Galahad, and I will show you.'

Nimbly and excitably, he set off down the stairs and along a corridor. I followed him, feeling more irritated than curious.

'Shush!' said he, stopping and holding up his finger outside a door. 'You must creep in here very quietly.'

Gently he opened the door and entered, and I tiptoed in behind. The room was dark save for a single light from a lancet window, flinging a beam upon this most fair of mortal creatures. She was lying under doeskin covers and her face was startling, angelic, and framed by dark red hair stretched across the pillows like fire snakes. She was deep in sleep and her snowy bosom did a delicate wave-motion with each unhurried breath.

'By the Holy Rood,' said I, 'I would rather her than a brass dish of water and a dozen eggs.'

'You always had good taste, Galahad,' said Sir Bors.

'Sir Galahad,' said Juliet Bors. 'You have the reputation of being the purest and noblest of all the knights. I am sure such a reputation is not unfounded.'

I quaffed my seventh goblet of strong red wine and replied. 'Madam, purity is a quality that tarnishes with time. None of us are perfect and I, like other knights, have been sorely tempted to break my most solemn vows. One has to weigh the prize against the length of time one might have to spend in purgatory.'

The damsel drew back from me slightly. 'That is a cynical remark, Sir Galahad. Is this what they preach in the chapels of Camelot?' She fluttered her eyelids. 'How incredibly wicked!'

'Well my sweet,' said Sir Bors, putting his arm around her waist. 'Galahad has been through the wars. He has seen the bad side of men as well as the good. One cannot criticise the hard-won wisdom of a veteran knight-errant.'

A messenger boy entered with a roll of parchment. He handed it to Sir Bors who read it slowly and frowned.

'Confound it!' he exclaimed, throwing the letter down. 'I have to go to Dover to sort out business. At least three of those wretched Caen masons have not turned up, and I might have to seek local men.'

'I will have to leave on the morrow as well,' I told him. 'The Holy Grail, you know, cannot wait.'

Sir Bors nodded absentmindedly. 'Yes, Galahad. The rack of life keeps turning, and who is exempt from a stretching?'

'You will not find it lonely here, Madam, now that your good husband has left for a few days.'

'I have the servants. They will look after me.'

'Good, then I will saddle Larkspur and make ready to leave.'

'Sir Galahad.' There is a soft catching in her voice. Her eyes draw out my sympathy.

'Yes Madam.'

Juliet bit her pretty lip then gazed demurely at her clasped hands. 'I have a problem.'

'Madam,' said I. 'There need be no secrets. Tell me, and then I will say whether I can be of help.'

'You see,' she said distraught, 'I am afraid of being thought foolish.'

'Madam, fools are common currency. You will not stand out in any way.'

'You mock me, Galahad.'

'Pray tell your tell your tale, and make it quick.'

Juliet took a long breath and composed herself. 'Every morning,' she began, 'I like to go riding around my estate to see the young does and conies playing. But I am now frightened, and I dare not go to a certain place. I have not told Sir Bors – he would merely laugh at me. But I have to confide in someone. Last month, I rode my horse up the hill above the copse. There is a level piece of ground on top and a small pond where waterfowl breed. It was my custom to get off my horse, let him drink, while I would watch the ducklings play. Well, on that fateful day, I was kneeling down by the pond, throwing crumbs to the birds, when I felt this hot deep breath rushing against my neck. Turning, I saw saw this most savage red dragon with black eyes. Screaming, I ran but he came after me, his long tail swishing and streaming in the air. His teeth were large and white and smelt of incense, and I was terror-struck.'

'What did you do?' said I.

Juliet lifted her polished bare shoulders and spread out her hands. 'I hid in the trees, of course. What else could I do?'

'I do not believe in dragons,' I told her forcefully. 'Juliet, these are modern times. Why, out there you find men living in good mud huts with pigs and cows and nice rush floors. They draw water up with iron buckets and heat food over fires. Dragons belong to our dark past. The last one was the Hydra, slain by Hercules aeons back.'

'There, I said you would mock me.'

'But, wait Juliet. I am prepared to visit your pond and linger awhile and see if anything appears.'

The next morning I rode up to the drinking-pool on Larkspur and watched the waterfowl skitter on the bright surface. After eight hours, I saw no sign of any dragon but met the woodcutter who worked on the estate. He was broken-veined and fiery in complexion, the colour of the dragon, and I wondered whether Juliet, in her nervous terror, had not foolishly mistaken him for the object of her fear. I asked the woodcutter whether he had seen a dragon.

'It's not for me to say, sir. Is it?'

I felt annoyed, discerning a gloating humility of tone. 'Course it is for you to say. I'm asking you. Have you seen any dragons?'

'Thinking of your reputation, sir? Are you?'

'What do you mean?'

'Well, sir, a knight who's dispatched a dragon – well he's the bat's hat, if you follow my meaning, sir.'

'Silence varlet!' I roared. 'The lady of this estate, Juliet Bors, has been frightened at this very spot by a red dragon. Do you know anything about it?'

The man pulled in his lower lip and brooded. 'It could be the Vikings, sir – I mean the sea pirates.'

'What are you talking about? They look like men.'

'I know that, sir,' he said. 'I am not stupid, you know. I was thinking of their ships which are carved like dragons at the prow.'

'What,' I asked, 'would a Viking vessel be doing a hundred miles inland? You cannot sail a ship up a hill and through a wood!'

'Well,' he said, hanging his head, 'I wouldn't know, not being nautical.'

Feeling that I was not pursuing a tangible beast, only something engendered by fear and fancy, I returned to Juliet and found her looking pale and anxious in one of the chambers at the back of the castle. She was lying on a couch and fanning herself. Her dress was of green silk embroidered at the edges with seed-pearl trefoils. One leg was arched up showing the fluent curve of her calves.

'I found no dragon up by the pool,' I told her.

'He is very cunning,' she replied. 'Today I was playing my flute in the garden, and I heard him steal up to me. Again I felt his breath rasp against my neck. Then I turned and saw his red tail lashing, and I ran back to my bedchamber and locked the door.'

'Did he appear again?' I asked.

'No, when I came out, he had gone.'

I placed my hands on her shoulders and looked into her eyes. 'Tomorrow I will wait in the garden.'

Enclosed by a golden Hamstone wall, the garden was extensive with a bell-shaped dovecote, vine-wreathed arbours and plots that brimmed with scented herbs, shivering willows and lemon flowers. Like an Eden of the mind, warm and mild and full of sweet growing things, yet walking there, I sensed a deadness. But still I trod lightly amid the blossoms, admired the silver fish in the pools and the statues of Venus and Eros beside the grotto. But I saw no sign of any dragon, only the gardener who was young and friendly. Crouching on his his knees, he was plucking weeds from the herb-beds. When I walked up to him, he smiled and offered me a large yellow pear.

Thanking him, I took the fruit. 'You have seen no dragon?' I asked.

'I have seen several, flying and flying. Look – there are two now!'

He pointed to a bright belt of air above the flower-beds. Long thin bodies hovered and dived, shimmering emerald and bright blue.

'The dragonflies are beautiful,' I murmured.

Leaving the gardener, I decided that this time I would be firm with Juliet. I found her sitting at a table in the refectory inhaling from a small dish containing attar of rose and clove. Seeing me, she smoothed down her long red gown and looked dismayed.

'Juliet, there is no dragon,' I told her harshly. 'I have sat in the garden all day, and no monster has interrupted my relaxation.'

'Sir Galahad,' said she, her eyes wide, 'you saw nothing in the garden because the serpent has changed his lair. Today I went to the chapel to pray. After the priest had left, I knelt down and closed my eyes, recited the catechism, and then I felt his warmth driving into me again. His white teeth glinted like lightning and his black eyes sought out the depths of my soul. His skin was all enflamed and his mouth open wide. He would have liked to have swallowed me there and then, but I escaped through the back door.'

'I will look into this matter for the last time,' said I. 'Then I must go.'

'I am grateful for your company, Galahad.'

'Do you yearn for gold?' I asked stopping by the door.

'Why do you ask?' She looked up surpised

'Dragons guard gold,' I told her. 'To see them may mean that you desire wealth.'

'I have too much gold,' answered she. 'My wealth is my prison.'

Next morning I visited the priest at the chapel who showed me round the small neat building. I admired the altar with its new silver crucifix studded with beryls. The carvings that decorated the elm seats were done with gusto: monkeys stealing grapes, men fishing, jugglers, a windmill, a stag, a hairy man bracketed with leaves.

Before I left, I spoke to the chantry priest. 'Surely no dragon ever comes here.'

'Indeed,' said he. 'This is a dragon chapel. It is dedicated to St. Margaret of Antioch. Do you not know the story?'

I shook my head.

'Margaret,' he told me, 'was brought up a Christian but she went to work under a man called Olybius, who did not respect her religion. Because she was beautiful, he had evil designs on her – but she was too pure to succumb to his advances. To avenge himself, he had her thrown in prison on a trumped-up charge. And there the Devil appeared to her in the form of a dragon. He opened his enormous jaws and actually swallowed Margaret, but such was her holiness that he was unable to digest her. She broke out of the monster's stomach and was delivered.'

'A fine tale and well told,' I murmured, feeling that I had the anwer.

Leaving the chapel, I wandered into the garden and inhaled the summer scents and sounds. Then I sat down and thought long and hard.

That night, to prepare myself for combat, I washed and anointed my body with precious oil and stood before the window in my shirt. Before me, on the mantle, a terrible red face glowered with black eyes, affronted nostrils and curved and shining fangs. Taking up the grotesque mask that I had forged, I placed it over my head and picked up my sharp sword.

I heard footsteps going up the stairs to the bedroom. Their patterings faded and a door shut. Leaving my chamber, I followed their echoes until I came to the room with the panelled oak door. It was unlocked. I entered quietly. Juliet was waiting for me in a thin grey silk gown. I stood before her in my distorted guise. She let out a small scream and her hands fluttered to her face.

'I am the monster that you have long desired,' I announced, taking off the mask.

Ice and fire were struggling in my veins. I raised the sword, brought it down. Two quick cuts above the shoulders, the silken gown fell away like misty water from pale white rock. I gazed upon her naked, trembling body, with her bare breasts lovelier than the twin moons of Jupiter. I placed my arms around her, cupping her warm white buttocks with my hands, and drew her in. And then, indeed, I felt it, the dragon, the old serpent, the wily cunning one. He was rising and calling and searching for his lair in the thicket. And then, yes, by the Holy Rood, he found it!

'Galahad, what are you doing here?'

The voice falls over me like a shock of water – the fire is quenched!

Turning, I size up the portly bulk of Sir Bors in the doorway. His eyes were angry buds of blue and his face dark and clenched. Juliet picked up a doeskin cover and moved over to the window.

'Still looking for the Holy Grail,' I replied.

# 9

# AND SO TO BATH

Ride Larkspur, ride.' Crouching forward, I urged Larkspur to break into gallop. A fine mare, swift as a swallow on the winds of spring, her hooves plunged over the sloping sward of downland. A surge of pleasure quickened my veins as the air beat my cheeks and my mind was borne aloft with the flying clouds. How galloping lifts one's spirits! The soul soars and forgets the petty cares and altercations that bedevil the thinking man.

Sir Bors' voice still echoed in my ears. 'Never darken my drawbridge again, Galahad!' he had shouted. 'Never darken my drawbridge again.'

Naturally his whole attitude was tainted by jealous rage. Sodding Oddbods! It was he who had first shown me Juliet – thinly gowned and lying asleep in her bedchamber to boot! Did Bors expect me to be satisfied with eye-lust alone? Faith, I am not a monk but Galahad, a knight of fair to middling purity, and I simply cannot deny myself those small luxuries that add a twinkle to the Dark Ages.

Easing into a walking-pace, I steadied Larkspur and took her up a long, smooth slope that came out on the shoulder of a hill, near a place called Roughthorn Farm, marked by one stark tree prodding the horizon. Then I saw two figures – struggling, so far as I could make out, against the solitary trunk. Wait! They were not just two men, but a man and a woman. By Jupiter, nasty business afoot!

A bearded red-haired oaf was pinning a young and slender maid to the tree. His outspread arms bound her to the bark, and she was struggling, kicking and biting. Her blue robe was bushed up around her thighs, partly masked by his hairy legs. 'A little wildcat, aren't you?' he chuckled. 'That's right, beauty, claw away, have a good spit and scratch! All the blood and sweat – t'will make a fine bonding-glue.'

Flinging myself off Larkspur, I grabbed hold of him and yanked him away and said with brisk civility,'I do not think the lady desires your attentions.'

Swinging round he glared, an insolent face with quick blue eyes, a thin, trembling mouth. 'Well, what have we here?' he sneered. 'A knight, all done up like the sunset with elbow-plates.'

'True, I like to keep a good shine on my armour,' I replied. 'Others might try polishing their manners.'

A flicker of a grin deepened the line of his mouth. 'Where's your beard?' he asked. 'Not man enough to grow one, I'll warrant. Or perhaps I'm looking at your rump. Prithee, tell me, gallant knight, what is thy arse doing on thy shoulders?'

Enraged, I smote the side of his head with my gauntlet. He drew in his breath and feigned amazement. 'What was that? Did the wing of a fairy brush my ear?'

'Be silent!' I commanded. 'Your mouth is as big as Ochy Hole and as full of foolish airs.'

Sneering, and with lazy casualness, he slipped out a knife from his belt, drawing the flat of the blade over his palm. The maid let out a cry and backed away. I held my ground, saying, 'My, what a pretty bauble! What do you intend to do with it? Cut out your tongue, I hope, so that we may be spared your wit for once and all.'

Lifting the blade above my head, he cried, 'No, this wicked little point is designed to carve pretty patterns on the face – sorry, the arse – of a knight who meddles in my affairs.'

He brought the knife down. Striking out my arm as a fend, I blocked the blow and butted his belly with my helmeted head. He bent over howling and clutching himself like a woman about to give birth. Locking my gauntlets prayer-wise, I raised them high and slammed them down against the back of his neck. He collapsed like a broken post, and I planted my heel on his head.

'There you are, where you belong, down among the worms and sheep's droppings.'

'So what?' he grunted, spitting out earth. 'You have the training and skill to belittle me with words and defeat me in combat. And now you've got the maid, but what will you do? Smarm her with gifts and Latin poems, but your object will be as base as mine: to break into that little chapel under her skirts.'

'My man,' I replied, 'I am a knight bound by the most solemn vows of chastity, which I only break when the urgency of a maiden's desires moves my heart to pity.'

'And how often, pray, is your heart moved to pity? Three times a night and once again at mid-day after a pitcher of wine and a few slices of red beef.'

'Silence!' I yelled, furious at the varlet's insolence. Dragging him up, I prodded him forward with my sword to a point fifty yards away, where there was a large Knucker Hole brimming with chill green water. 'There you go!' I lavished on him a mighty kick. 'The water will cleanse your mind and mouth.'

'Thank you, sir knight, for your swiftness and gallantry. I dare not dwell on what might have happened had you not intervened.'

The oaf had waddled off after a good deep ducking, and I had refreshed myself with a draught of wine. The maid was now regarding me, wary-eyed and pale after the ordeal. Her hair was a dishevelled riot – as if each separate strand was planning on taking flight – but her manner was reserved. With a look of bruised fortitude, she sat beside the pool with her head bowed and hands gripping her knees. Her green sash gown, worn after the Roman fashion, was badly torn, but she seemed to have regained some of her composure.

'Make no mention of it, Madam,' said I. 'A maiden in distress is one of the rare delights afforded by my vocation. And it is made doubly pleasurable when the lady chooses to express her gratitude in a certain way.'

'Is not the very act of performing a virtuous deed reward in itself?'

'Madam, I replied, though praise is lavished on virtuous maidens and men who take religious vows, few actually live out such a creed unless forced to, owing to bad luck or gross deformity. A man's life may be pure because he is ugly or lives in the frozen north where there are few wenches worth risking a sword or sonnet for. And think, is not virtue a kind of summons? If one sees a fresh field of snow, one does not gaze at it starstruck for hours. No, one goes out and treads in it until it is glorious mire of patterns and footprints. No, men do not love purity and virtue so much as the thought of tarnishing it. And that is why your uncouth attacker acted as he did.'

Why did I say such a thing – a minute after a man had tried to despoil her? Why do I have this doltish urge to make statements of outrageous boldness quite out of odds with my intentions? As soon as spoke, I saw her draw up her shoulders in an affronted way.

'I cannot reward you with my body, sir knight,' she returned briskly. 'But my father, King Bladud of Bath, and my stepmother, Queen Flavia, will be pleased to welcome you with payment and hospitality.'

'Bath is some fifty miles hence. What are you doing out here alone?'

'When I set out, I had a trusted companion with me – a man servant – but he was taken with the sickness and is presently being tended. So I carried on alone to the house of the friend. I'd almost done the journey when that brute set on me, making my horse bolt, and now I've no means of getting back to my father's court.'

'Madam,' said I. 'Though you refuse to transport me to delight with a certain favour, I am quite happy to perform the more menial mode of carriage by taking you to Bath.'

A pause and then she asked. 'What is your name, sir knight?'

'Galahad,' said I.

'I have heard of you. You have a most unblemished reputation.'

'You must not believe all you hear,' said I.

'I certainly do not. But I have heard that you once did some great deed. Wasn't it you who sat on a certain chair?'

That pinched my pride a little. But knowing it was not possible to control the shapes and hues of rumour, I answered civilly.

'Madam, I am a man bedevilled – that four-legged object is tied to my reputation like a monkey's tail! Yes, I have sat on the Siege Perilous many many times – after all, it is my chair! – but take no especial credit for it. I take far more pride in helping a beauty like yourself.'

Instantly she averted her face, as if my too-easy flattery strained her patience, and quickly I asked, 'And how shall I address you?'

'Catherine,' she replied with a trace of a smile. 'The name was my late mother's choice, for my father had no time for religion. The holy virgin martyr was much-esteemed in the year of my birth.'

'Holiness and virginity! Do women flaunt such banners to drive men mad?'

'Men are always finding something to be crazy over,' said she. 'There are some who spend all their days polishing swords and weapons, and others who are always changing their horses, thinking that the new steed will run faster. Then there are the bull-worshippers who crouch under grids and let blood leak all over their naked bodies – as if that will make them nobler! No, Sir Galahad, pray do not blame women, just because they do not offer themselves at the going rate. Man's madness is part of his birthright. He daren't cast it off, else he would find nothing useful to do.'

Her vehemence made me silent. I had judged her wrongly and decided to shrink myself a little to allow her to breathe and perceive all the more naturally. And maybe, in that less influencing atmosphere, she would be drawn towards me of her own accord. We can but hope. So instead of prattling, I found some good grazing ground for Larkspur and prepared the camp.

'We will have to enter the palace by the back,' said Catherine. 'My father is not popular in the town. He has too many creditors.'

We had just ridden through the gates of Bath, passing first an earth and then a stone rampart, followed by a broad muddy green where peasants were amusing themselves, pig-racing and running with their feet in bags. Then came the cock-pit, a huddle of hovels, and finally the core of the Roman town.

Four fluted columns of the temple reared up like mighty trunks of stone upholding a triangular pediment adorned with carvings of winged victories and of the goddess Minerva. A centrepiece showed the savage head of a male Gorgon, moustachioed like a warrior, with staring eyes and a stern mouth. The temple presided like a lion over the square. A proud, conquering statement, it made grubby unheroic midgets of the artisans and commoners scurrying around like worker ants and dwarfed the dusty cart-rutted streets, all aglint with boggy pools made by the packhorse ponies, which heaved to and fro laden with wool-bales and tin-ingots from the Mendips.

I turned to Catherine. 'I thought the temple had fallen, sacked by the invaders.'

'It was my father's ambition to rebuild it, to raise the ruins from the mud. And that is what he did, bankrupting himself in the process, and now he is hated and despised.'

Dismounting, Catherine pulled her riding hood over her face and made towards a side door. A group of men were congregating on the temple steps, traders and craftsmen by their looks, clad in blue and grey woollens and leather jerkins. One man with a pugnacious face was saying, 'I worked a full six months for Bladud, sawing and planing and lugging the stones from the quarries. I paid him with sweat and blood, and what did I get in return? Dribs and drabs, and now, what with the plague in the villages, there is not enough clean food and water.'

Taking my arm, Catherine took me down an arcaded corridor and stopped outside a large door. 'Wait here,' she said. She went through into a vaulted room and not long after came out, saying. 'You may enter, Galahad, and speak to father. I will change my clothes and meet you later.' With a quick smile, she hurried away. I stepped through into a tall and splendid room. Bronze shafts of light slanted down from long thin windows, spilling a largesse of radiance upon rich, dusky tapesties and a floor made comfortable by the cured skins of young bullocks. At the far end, seated on a oak chair with a winged backpiece, King Bladud cut a regal figure. Tall, swaggering and handsome with shaggy gold locks, his blue eyes, restless and brooding, like one whose true thoughts were kept in hiding.

When I walked up to him, I was taken aback to see that he had a pink piglet snuffling around his knees, which was clad in a little scarlet cape with gold thread at the edges and a silver collar inscribed with the name Taranis. Bladud pushed an apple into the creature's mouth and smiled. 'Taranis is my most intelligent courtier, moderate in his habits, though his eyesight is not excellent and he tends to nip one's toes.'

Bending, I stroked the animal which at least was clean. 'The Druids,' I observed, 'hold pigs sacred.'

Bladud gave an affirmative grunt. 'So I understand. They confer swine-like qualities upon their gods. They also believe that they can change the course of the stars by preparing a mixture of belladonna and rosemary and mumbling incantations over it?'

'I cannot comment, sire,' said I. 'I know nothing of astronomy. Doubtless, should such methods work, life would be less intractable.'

Bladud rose from his seat and took my hand firmly. 'Galahad, forgive me such distractions, when I should be thanking you. Let me say how grateful I am that you should offer Catherine help when she was in need. Naturally, my palace and entourage is at your disposal for as long as you wish to stay. I know that you are from the court of Arthur, a man I respect, although I think him wrong-headed, chasing Grails and relics, but then there is the small boy in all of us.'

'I agree, sire. What use is it, a chalice that floats about in a golden cloud?'

Bladud observed calmly. 'I have heard that the Grail was the cup used by the Risen One.'

I nodded. 'The vessel out of which he drank before his death.'

Bladud frowned and lowered his gaze. I could see pondering the subject of the Grail was not to his taste, and he abandoned the effort with a shrug declaring, 'So my fine knight, you are left pursuing the imprint of a crucified man's lips.' He threw back his shoulders – robust laughter spread and echoed. 'Ghosts, shadows, tinctures of the dead – that is the stuff of faith! But be of good heart, Galahad. Remember, the chase is finer than the kill.'

I barely knew him. Yet already I felt dominated by his unpredictable swerves of discourse. And then, taking hold of my arm, he said, 'Come, I will show you the palace.'

Leaving the state-room, he took me down a steep staircase. Wafts of steam and burning tar snipped my breath short at the bottom. The sharp, wet odour was coming through a square-cut passage which Bladud entered. I followed him along and down some more steps and the heat became intense – as if the building was sweating like a beast. More steps followed, slippery and uneven, leading down – for aught I knew – to the very pit of Hades. At one point, when Bladud stopped, I almost suspected a trap, then he turned and gestured at me.

'Here,' he said, 'is an exposed artery of the earth whose heart feeds all volcanoes and molten rivers.'

I stopped and gazed. There was a hot dark arch under which warm water gushed out from a spring and reservoir. It slipped over a ledge of blood-red stone and down a lead-lined conduit. Steam, iron-flavoured and billowing, arose and cooled in the air above, streaming down the coursed walls. I noted the word 'Sulis' crudely carved in the rock.

Bladud anticipated my question. 'Sulis – he is the native god of the throbbing spring. When the Romans built the temple, they gave it a dual dedication, coupling his name with that of Minerva. Both preside over water and its curative properties.'

'Where does the heat come from?' I asked.

'From deep in the earth's core,' replied Bladud. 'It is molten down there. Some men say it is because dragons breed in the bowels of the earth, heating all the water that arises to the surface. But I do not believe that. I think that the heart of the earth is all raging fire and minerals, and that acts upon the water that is stored above, forcing it up through gaps in the rock, so that it gushes forth when its reaches the surface.'

'Why have you thrown so much of your life into restoring the baths?'

'When I was a young man,' said Bladud, 'I was marked out as gifted, handsome and erudite. I was a king's son and my future was secure. But then one day, a white spot appeared on my arm, and my father, King Ludhudibras, was forced to banish me from the court. I had become infected with leprosy – all men shunned my company. I took up employment as a swineherd, in which capacity I was competent, but then one day, to my horror, I found that sores were appearing on the pigs. They were squealing and sickening. I did not know what to do, and then one of the boars sighted this vast mound of acorns by the River Avon. It began running towards it and the rest of the herd followed, flinging themselves into the water, which seemed to be steaming at that point. When they had finished eating, they came out and their sores seemed to have cleared. Curious, I decided to follow their example, bathing in the warm waters, and when I emerged I felt better. So I visited the warm pool every day, until my leprosy was healed, and I was able to return to the court of my father. Later I traced the outfall to its source by the Roman ruins, and I decided that I would make it my life's work to rebuild the glory and grandeur of Rome.'

'So pigs were your early mentors.'

Bladud nodded. 'Now I will show you the communal baths, used by my courtiers and attendants.'

Turning, he led me past a small underground temple, with walls inset with skulls and shells, to another flight of narrow steps. They led up to a spacious stone corridor adorned by busts of deceased emperors with brows like bears and noses like eagles.

'Here is my masterpiece,' said Bladud.

The corridor emerged into the immense space of the lead-sheeted baths. I stopped and my mouth opened like a fish. For it was like being in a cathedral where steam swirled around instead of incense and gushing green water filled the nave and looming shafts of stone held up the ceiling. The scene was a busy one. There was a broad pavement around the water lined with stone seats and arcades, where palace vendors sold wine, bread and honey cakes. Naked men and women were cavorting in the waters. Others were playing at dice or exercising in the spaces between the arches. Directly I entered with King Bladud, a young woman, sparsely clad in a single oakleaf, came forward and offered us a tray on which there was green ginger and various comfits.

I took one but Bladud pushed out a dismissive hand at her and the overdressed courtiers who straightway moved back.

'These modern times do not suit my temper,' he explained. 'I am ill at ease with the prattlings and pretensions of the present. My tolerance is tried by whingeing wights who bear down on me with their protests and demands. The masons and stone-dressers want payment, payment for services rendered. So do the cooks and kitchen scullions and the smiths who work the metal! But look at this,' he gestured towards the curving splendour of the vaulted roof, 'I have raised up this magnificent monument. Is not that sight payment enough?'

'It is not payment when men go hungry.'

'True, but I am king and need to eat. Besides, my days are numbered. In time the mob will storm the palace larders and take all there is to eat. Do you know what they cry at night? Bladud, Bladud, bread or blood! Bread or blood!'

I shrugged. 'You cannot quell a mob by ignoring its demands when there is shortage and suffering.'

'Neither can you appease it when they hate you and all your works.'

'You are a king, sire, responsible to his people. They will be your judge.'

'How can they judge me?' asked Bladud. 'They have not an inkling of what moves my mind and stirs my soul. Is history a chronicle wherein lesser men pass sentence on the greater?'

'If they fail them, yes. You cannot have the privileges of a king without some of the responsibilities.'

I forced the words out, but did not attend to Bladud's response. For an unfamiliar weakness was dragging through my limbs. Perhaps the onslaught of steam and heat was raising vile humours in me. I tried to steady myself but found that I barely had the strength to clench my fingers. Swaying, I reached for one of the pillars. Bladud did not notice but continued to extol his self-centred virtues. I was sagging like a wet leaf. My veins seemed to be filled with thin water. My knees shook. I fell forward, struck my head, and saw a shock of stars amid a flowering black.

For ten days and nights I suffered, afflicted by a most cruel fever. I lay in an agony of grey, sweating skin and trembling fingers. Other times I would plunge into a sleep, so deep and wild that I did not expect ever to return. At night visions rose before me: King Cealwin sprawled in his trough of blood grinning, the Grail whirling round his head his like a golden bird; the kindly face of Juliet Bors; and Arthur himself, looking noble yet distant in pale green robes embroidered with swords and skulls.

Arthur became transparent and faded out. He was replaced by fantastic forms: female bodies with swans' necks and heads of goats, sea-horses arising from the foam, and a black bull with a single golden horn stuck in its forehead. It charged at me, bellowing like the Devil in chains, and I turned and twisted in my sheets. But then an arm caught hold of me and smoothed my brow.

Opening my eyes, I saw Catherine, kind-faced, attentive, pounding herbs in a pestle. Light from the lancet window slanted in, lending a golden glow to the pale stone of the sick-room.

'Bad dreams, Galahad?' Catherine murmured. 'You are passing through the dark night of the fever. Soon you will recover, and then you will be able to continue your quest.'

'I am tired of Grails and goals,' I told her. 'I seek only rest and contentment.'

Catherine gave a wan smile. 'You will not find it in this life, Galahad. And you would spurn it if you did.'

'Since you have been my nurse, Catherine, I have felt very close to you. I want to become part of you.'

She trickled a little more water into the pestle and ground the herbs with extra force. 'That is not possible. Unless you would wish the surgeon to stitch us together like a pair of freaks.'

'You know my meaning. You laugh at me for having deep feelings.'

'Galahad,' said she, straightening my blankets, 'I know all about your feelings. They may be deep but their duration is seldom more than a day.'

'If you will not accept my love,' I told her, 'I will hasten to the monastery and garb myself in sackcloth and ashes.'

'The monastery in Bath,' she retorted, 'is full of cardsters and gamesters and lapsed penitents. Far better join the hospital to look after the lepers and those with the pox.'

Her voice, detached yet comforting, dwindled into mist and distance. The terrible sinking sickness gripped me again. And as I was drawn down into its murky coils, from somewhere beyond that light-filled room, I heard noises, sullen cries, commotion in the street, followed by the chant, 'Bladud – bread or blood! Bladud – bread or blood!'

'Poor father,' murmured Catherine. 'The mob will get him in the end, and who shall live to remember all this folly and magnificence?'

Queen Flavia smiled at me across the feasting table. A tall mound of skinned pears covered in dried syrup stood between us. As I reached for one, clasping the round, sticky surface, she let out a little gasp and touched her breast with her palm, as if I were handling not the fruit but her warm skin.

Her signs were not the hardest to decipher, and I smiled at her whenever I could. For she was beautiful in a fair-skinned Celtic way, the opposite of her dark stepdaughter. Bladud's second wife had burnished copper hair, amber eyes and a cool, stately manner. I sensed in her a strength and single-mindedness that perhaps derived from a core of self-sufficiency. Like Catherine, she was aware of her charms, but different in that she used them to grasp at whatever possible pleasure lay at hand. Even her silences were the strategies of a coquette rather than time in which thoughts might settle and order themselves.

'You are now fully recovered from your sickness, Sir Galahad?' she asked. 'It is good to see you up and about after being bedridden for so long.'

'Sickness madam,' said I, 'brings its knowledge and insights. We learn how vulnerable is the clay of the body. At such times it cracks and shatters, flinging us against the very brink of mortality. We glimpse that chasm which will devour us all in time. And then a kindly nurse, like your stepdaughter, takes hold of the invalid and leads him up to the orchards of health. But the knowledge is there, of heaven, hell, extinction or extension – call it what you will.'

The Queen looked thoughtful. I took up a goblet of wine and mightily quaffed it down. It had been a most splendid banquet, with Bladud entertaining us in high Roman style. We had eaten a marvellous fare: pig garnished with cake and giblets, beetroot and wholemeal bread – not that awful white stuff! – and cold tart laced with warm honey followed by a potent Gallic wine.

Two seats down, Catherine was sitting, clad in a yellow sash gown, not long enough to hide her cherry-red petticoats, spiral anklets and white slippers embroidered with gold. I felt a smarting indignation; all her attention seemed to be reserved for a certain young man.

I turned to Queen Flavia. 'Where is your good husband, madam? He left the banquet early.'

The Queen looked downcast. 'Bladud is obsessed with his work in the laboratory. Nothing else matters to him – all his building projects are achieved.' She exhaled a wistful sigh. 'I did think once that to be married to a clever man would sustain my needs. But cleverness fails, for it is all bound up with itself. Sometimes I wished that Bladud might compliment me on my beauty, my singing voice, my dress, but all he cared for was astronomy, mathematics and flying things. Did you know that, on the night of our wedding, I was lying in my bedroom, feeling roused and ready to receive him. He entered wearing clean white and gold vestments and lay beside me, saying, 'Now I shall satisfy my lust with the fairest lady in all the land.' And then, quite suddenly, a butterfly darted into the bedchamber, red with black and yellow markings on its wings. Bladud sprang up and gave chase. It flitted behind the curtain, under an arch and down the stairs. He left me and began to run after it. All night I heard his feet, thumping and clattering, and in the morning he came into my room holding a little glass jar. I have it here, he said, a Red Maid of the Woods. Isn't it exquisite?'

'Madam,' said I, 'it is a great sadness that the things that stir us into loving another are often just those qualities that make them incapable of returning that same love.'

The Queen nodded. 'You speak wise words, Sir Galahad. You are a man of experience.'

'But though our deepest loves may fail us,' said I, 'it is still possible to enjoy a few easeful moments with a transient, a passing stranger, with whom one may reach a brief empathy.'

The Queen looked at me curiously. 'But you have your vows, Sir Galahad.'

'My vows,' said I, 'are made even more precious and solemn in the breaking. It would indeed be a harsh and vengeful God, who was not moved to pity by the sight of an lovelorn knight and a peerless queen who enjoys his companionship.'

The Queen gave me a pointed stare. 'Right', she hissed. 'Here are my plans. You are to meet me by the Roman baths at midnight, when Bladud retires to his laboratory, third alcove down from the entrance.'

I was disarmed by the swiftness of her response. It implied that this was not the first time she had arranged such trysts. But then, with knights of my ilk galloping around, that was no marvelling matter.

The water of the baths shone emerald and black in the light of the lanterns hanging from the colonnades. I waited for the Queen underneath the third alcove where the vendors traded during the day. A round glow blossomed like an orange beneath the arched entrance and wafted back and forth – someone was signalling her presence. Swiftly I moved up to greet the Queen who smiled and placed her lamp on the floor. She was wearing a tissue-thin gown, silver-trimmed and ending just below her knee. Advancing towards me with leisurely grace, I noted her glance, the amused anticipation of a veteran rather than the timorous flush of a virgin. I felt a warm fluttering inside. How full and lovely her flanks! How proud and finely contoured her breasts!

Swanning over the tiled way, she took my hand, drawing me beneath one of the lantern-lit arches. I looked out to the enormous dark lake of water, and she smiled and pointed to the wall behind.

'See,' she whispered. 'We are standing surrounded by the ghosts of dead lovers.'

I glanced to the wall. Roman graffiti was scratched out on the smooth blocks of honey stone:

*Figulus loves Idaia.*

*Fortunatus, you great fornicator, someone who knows you wrote this.*

*Venerusa, I hope you love him well.*

*Modestus had a tryst here with Albana.*

*Julius Promogrenius was here on time, what's keeping you?*

*I'm going off abroad now, goodbye my Sava, keep on loving me.*

I turned to the Queen. 'It is clear, madam, that the passions that moved them persist to this day.'

Smiling, she led me along the row of colonnades, stopping by a stone table where a small charcoal brazier glinted red and black. 'Lie there, Galahad,' she murmured. 'Take off your vestments, and I will treat you like a battle-weary centurion.'

I obeyed, removing what I had on, while the queen heated some small pans over the fire. A minute later she came over holding a jar of jessamine-scented oil. 'Lie still,' she told me, 'I will anoint you.'

I do not think that I have ever experienced a more perfect moment. The Queen dipped her hands into the jar and skimmed her palms over my chest, smoothing and spreading the warm amber oil, down along my arms, thighs and legs. Then she bade me turn over, and I obeyed. And again her hands, firm and pliant, pressed the oil deep into my muscles. At times her mouth swooped low, kissing the base of my spine, and then more oil would be applied, rippling and trickling down into my clefts, followed by the strong, probing fingers, stretching and kneading my skin, urging me on to wilder shores of sensation.

'And now,' she murmured, 'the cloak of gold.'

Taking up a handful of sand from a silver pail, she trickled a thin stream over my oiled body, until I was like a statue encrusted with glinting siliceous specks.

The Queen smiled. 'Now you are my own jewelled Adonis.'

'Faith,' said I. 'I itch like an ape.'

'Have patience,' she soothed.

Producing a kind of wooden knife, which she called a stygil, she scraped away the sand and oil. It was marvellous – what coarse, delicious friction! Yellow-brown particles yielded to the busy wooden blade, bunching in ridges and shrugging off, exposing my ever-increasing whiteness. As the sticky patches were removed, I emerged new-peeled and shining like Adam from the hand of God.

'Now,' she whispered, 'we will take the plunge together.'

I followed her to another room which had a bath with a carved stone fountain in the middle, decorated with a statue of Neptune who was riding upon a dolphin. A steaming jet of warm water surged from the dolphin's mouth, and the Queen and I jumped in and splashed around like sparrows in a puddle. When I put my arms around her, she moved away, saying. 'Not here, but in my bedchamber. Bladud will be working.'

I eased myself up in bed. Queen Flavia was beside me, folded securely in sleep. She had a smile on her lips as if dreaming of pleasant things. It is those that trust the world, I thought, who sleep easiest. They are like children who yield their all to the night, open and compliant. But when men turn into merchants and deceivers, they no longer sink easily into the lap of sleep, but toss and twist, keeping one nightmare eye open for the robbers and creditors who stalk about inside their skulls berating and demanding more.

As silvery beams flooded the chamber, I took in the sumptuous furnishings. The bed, all hung with white and silk linen, had a counterpane of gold, trimmed with ermine. The walls of the room were painted an imperial blue that seemed black in that light. I got out of bed and stared at the moon that shone with a vehemence that made me think of truth. I had performed that 'rite of night' Dylfric was wont to fume and shriek about and which broods and sweats over young men's dreams and makes them think of snares, she-devils and succubi. And yet, now it was over, I should have been calm and clear of mind. Usually by the act of passion, you are able to rise above it, but that night I was not granted that keen-sighted sense of ease.

As I stole out of the bedchamber, I thought of Catherine whom I had so lightly betrayed. I went cold and quaked a little. I shivered with shame. But then I thought: why should I think so? Sodding Oddbods! I had done nothing wrong. Catherine and I had not yet embraced. No promises or betrothals had been made. I had not asked a reward of her or her father. And yet I felt my impious snatch at a fleeting pleasure – with her stepmother to boot! – was more likely to set her against me than draw us closer. I was therefore determined that she should not learn of it. If one chooses to confess, what is one doing? Filling the mind of another with the grits, muds and treacherous glues, the foul secretions deriving from one's own ignoble acts. To share – or make a clean breast of – is also to contaminate another. No one deserves that. To linger with one's shames in silence is more stoic and honourable. Besides, the only person I had truly betrayed was my host, King Bladud, and I was hardly likely to confront him.

I slipped down the corridor, as quietly as I could, but as I tiptoed along, I became aware of a dim, flickering light that made my passage ahead easier. From where did it come? Then I heard a pursuing breath behind, a light panting, and turned to face whoever it was.

'Galahad!' cried the King, holding a lantern up to my face. 'What are you doing? You have just come out of the Queen's bedchamber.'

'I beg your indulgence, sire,' said I, shamefaced and trembling, for the Queen had convinced me that he would not be about at this hour. 'But I have been deep in thought this past hour and have paid scant attention to my whereabouts.'

'Aha!' said he, slapping my back and leading me by the arm along the corridor. 'We are two of a kind, Galahad. You pacing about all night, dwelling on your vows and not knowing your own quarters from my good lady's room, and I pondering the problems of science and philosophy. Thinking men, you see, who have no time for the tusslings and distractions that afflict the common folk. Their talk is all of eating, drinking and bedding willing maids. But you and I, Galahad, have our minds fixed on higher things. We wish to get to grips with those intangible forces that direct our destinies.'

I nodded nervously. 'Sire, you have plumbed the depths of my character admirably.'

'By the way,' he added, 'did you find Queen Flavia a satisfactory adulteress?'

Even I was unable to answer that. I stared down at my boots and gave a dull cough.

But Bladud laughed and spread out his hands in a gesture of indifference. 'It is all right, Galahad. I was jesting. I saw it at the start – that you, essentially, are a besieger of boudoirs! If that is your calling, you may as well pursue it as ably as Destiny intended. I pass no censure because I have lost all interest in such matters. My first wife, Julia, pined away because of my inattention and died soon after giving birth to Catherine. Queen Flavia is made of sturdier stuff. She finds recompense in lovers, while I go about my work, which is all I truly care about.'

'What are your researches, sire?'

'I will show you. Later, I will need your assistance.'

Striding swiftly, he led me to a small ante-room beneath the baths. From there we crawled through a hole and entered a labyrinth of dank passages. Bladud bolted down the largest of these which came out by a flight of stone steps. 'Up here,' he muttered and began to climb with perilous rapidity. I followed with caution, grimly clutching on to lengths of chain and rope run down the length of the way. Steep, slippery in places and littered with sawn-off blocks of stone, they were jagged and hazardous. But the King bounded up them with antelope ease. Being perpetually on horseback, I was less used to such Olympian effort and had to slow my breathing and contain my pace until my strength revived. Keeping my eyes fixed on the tail-light of the King's lantern, my senses gradually shaped themselves to naught but rock and shadow. Over an hour passed in which we never uttered a single word.

Finally we finished climbing, emerging into a hood-shaped cavern from which a stone corridor branched out. Bladud went down this and entered another enclosure at the end. By now, I wished to rest but was forced along by his unrelenting energy. 'See here,' he called, 'the very heart of the mystery – my laboratory!'

We stepped inside a stone chamber with a big iron furnace blazing at one end. On the walls were chalked configurations of the zodiac and drawings of a winged dragon, a sea urchin, a pair of conjoined scallops, triangles, discs and measurements. All around, stacked against the walls, were glass jars containing feathers and quills of every size and colour, specimens of insects, flying creatures and a collection of eggs, ranging from tiny blue things, scarcely bigger than beads, to marbled monsters as big as urns. On a bench in the centre was a set of tools: iron needles, blades and knives of different shapes and a speculum for polishing lenses.

Eyeing me fiercely, the King picked up a large jar, unscrewed it and took something out. 'Do you know what this is, Galahad?' he asked.

He held it up to my view, a moist muscled lump, pink-red in colour, with blue veins all over it.

'It is a human heart,' said the King. 'I cut it out of a dead man in order to extract a certain blue pigment that I needed.'

He laughed brutally, showing mica-white teeth, and tossed the heart into the furnace. It hissed and hardened in the flames; a veil of steam arose and thinned to nothing.

'I have no heart, Galahad,' the King raged. 'No heart at all, merely a spirit.'

'Such distinctions perplex me, sire.'

'The heart is all about love, hate and passion,' Bladud declared. 'But the spirit is concerned with exactitude, fervour and mathematics.'

Striding up to an alcove beside the furnace, Bladud drew back a black silk curtain. A square of blinding blue light drummed against my eyeballs. I moved forward blinking, feeling the intoxicating rush of clean air against my face. I gasped, realising how high we had climbed, far up above the mines, then higher still, into the summits of the hills. I was gazing out over a precipice from where I was able to identify the greens and public buildings of Bath outspread beneath the dawn mist. Smoke was hanging in a pall above the stagnant air of the valley, and I could make out the shape of the Roman temple and the river, like a twisting silver serpent, crawling through a wooded valley up towards the port of Brigstow. Above us, the larks were urging in the summer and the scent of morning wind soothed and lightened my mood.

Bladud glared at the rising sun. 'If earth is the element of the heart,' he said, 'then air is the domain of the spirit. Up here in the sky are the palaces of the gods. From this height, you can look down on the town, and it appears tidy, neat, contained, a radiating pattern of lines, arcs and squares – all is form and geometry.'

'Distance confers an illusion of order and tranquility,' said I. 'But the mud of life will always cling to our boots, however far removed our preoccupations from the commonplace.'

'I disagree.' Bladud turned. 'Permit me to show you the means whereby I will exalt myself above the clods and clergy.' He went back under the archway, waited for me to follow, then drew back the curtain, taking a corridor leading upward. I trailed along and found myself in another large room carved out of the golden rock.

'Show me the commonplace in this,' Bladud challenged. 'And I will indeed be amazed.'

Spread across the room, which was really a large workshop, was a massive pair of wings mounted on a wheeled carriage. Like an immense bodiless bird, it lay poised and perfect, light gusts from outside trembling the feathers. Fitted to it at strategic points were wrist-cuffs and leg-straps and tiny flaps and flanges, all inter-locking and pinned with nails. Struts and tendons of bamboo formed the support-ing frame and the leather parts were waxed to a sheen. I might have dismissed Bladud as mad, but the fine detail of the workmanship, the precision and symme-try, belied such a view.

'You have heard of Icarus,' he said.

'The sun melted his wings and he drowned in the Aegean.'

'That is not the fate I have planned for myself,' said Bladud. 'Attend to me, Galahad. At midnight, I want you to open the gates of the palace and let in the mob.

They will raid the cold caves, where the food is stored, take their share of loot, no doubt, and desecrate the baths and temple. I have arranged for the Queen to be accomodated at a monastery, while I want you to ensure the safety of my daughter, Catherine. Take her as far as Cirencester, where relatives will attend to her welfare. You see, Galahad, I still care for people a little.'

'And yourself?' I asked.

Bladud pointed at the dawn sky. 'I will fly into whatever awaits me up there. I will find out whether or not the gods dwell in the heavens. Perhaps I will even become one. Who knows what transformations will take place once man is relieved of his earthly anchor?'

The sand-clock had almost run to the mark. It was time for me to confront the mob, who were ranged outside the temple steps, still crying for the blood of the King.

When I went out, a great cry arose. A few quarry-workers, armed with chisels and hammers, surged forward as if to attack. But I stood my ground, flashing my sword towards their chests, saying, 'Good people, hold back and listen. I am going to unlock the gates. The larders of the palace are yours for the taking. The King extends to you his apologies for not being present, but trusts that you will not be too grief-stricken by his absence.'

I sheathed my sword. A mason came towards me brandishing an iron mallet, but I slunk away into the darkness, elbowing past the milling horde, cutting a wedge through to the tiny courtyard by the side of the temple. There Larkspur and another horse, saddled and laden with provisions, were waiting.

Catherine was prepared and ready, clad in her red woollen riding cloak. Her eyes were stern and cool. Briskly she climbed upon her mount and urged it forward.

'We must ride hard,' said I. 'While we are in the land of the living.'

We galloped out through the city gates and up into the hills. When we had ridden for an hour, it was time for the horses to rest and drink. Catherine helped me light a fire, and we sat beside each other, staring into the spritely flames, our breath flowing even and unhurried. Despite a feeling of grateful deliverance, I was not at ease. There was commotion in my head – too much for any form or order to establish itself. I wanted to stay with what was happening and see it through, but knew that was not possible.

Catherine poked the fire with a stick. 'What will happen to the temple?'

'It will be sacked and destroyed in a day,' said I.

She gazed into the flames and frowned. 'Poor father. It was hardly worth it.'

'Time makes ruins of man and all his works,' said I. 'And if you take the long view, a hundred years and a day are much the same.'

'They are not the same, Galahad. In the first, a man can live a full life, see through his children and descendants, but in the second he can scarcely take breath before he is no more.'

'Yes, but the end of both is the same.'

'Your emphasis is false and levelling,' Catherine cut across, 'being placed at the point a man or woman dies. Now if instead, you were to dwell on the living achievements, of my father and my mother, say, and not their common sharing of an end, you'd have a more inspiring story.'

Her words were interrupted by a series of muffled squeals. I rose and drew my sword. They were issuing from a blanket beside Catherine, and I was preparing to take on some fearsome creature of the night. But she picked up the small bundle and unwrapped it, revealing Bladud's pet piglet, Taranis, still clad in his scarlet coat and silver collar.

I threw down my sword and stroked the creature. 'You decided to retain the family mascot?'

'He would have been taken by the mob.'

'The courtiers are perhaps suffering such a fate at this very moment.'

'Who's a lucky piglet?' she murmured taking him in her lap.

I stared enviously at my pink-eyed, tulip-eared rival whose trotters and snout still looked amazingly clean. And then I said, 'Catherine, I have been asked by your father to escort you to Cirencester, where I believe you have relatives.'

'You are sure Father is safe?' she asked.

'As an experimenter, he is not much interested in safety,' said I. 'But he is fulfilling his destiny, not anybody else's, and that is surely worthwhile.' I picked up a pitcher and rose to my feet. 'I'll fetch some water.'

Catherine waited by the fire. I made my way to the spring inside a ring of trees and dipped the pitcher in the cold, flat water. Below, the bluff of the hilltop fell away steeply to a black valley, pricked out with rubies where men had lit camp fires and warning beacons. The moon was full, round and brilliant, and as I gazed I became aware of something moving across the sky.

Resembling a snowy owl, only a hundred times larger, it cleaved the dark spaces in long and fluent swoops, rose again and circled. No breeze stirred. It seemed the thing could use the rising air, floating with the currents and gliding evently. Like a small boat crossing a sea of cloudy troughs and crests, it charted a course towards the diamond of a faraway star. I was inspired to watch it, thinking, yes, it has broken the anchorage of earth and escaped into that absolutely pure domain, free of all gross substances, in which the harp of Apollo endlessly plays. But a little later, I was disillusioned. For I saw that ship of wonder start to stall, then weave crazily like a bird taken sick, and droop and sink earthwards. Did it plunge and break itself to sticks and fragments? Or did it rise and recover? I turned my eyes away, there being things which I prefer to leave unresolved, like visions and dreams that peter out in mist and darkness.

## 10

# THE THIEF

Trotting side by side with Catherine was pleasing. We ambled in many a shady vale and crossed many a fair stream. Sometimes she played a flute to ease the journey and her conversation was brisk and lively. I asked her what type of man she hoped to marry.

'He need not be rich,' she replied. 'Nor need he be handsome or quick of mind. Nor need he be religious. But I would like him to show kindness to all things.'

'What about wolves and tigers?' I asked. 'If he were kind to them, they might respond by feasting on his flesh.'

'You are too jocular, Galahad. You think yourself funny, and yet you make me want to slap you hard.'

'I live in hope,' said I.

Emerging from a valley, we cantered along by a broad meadow, where corn grew tall and apple and pear flourished. There was a large farm, with a tower at one end, and attached to it was a round dovecote, a duckpond, and many stables and barns. 'There is a wealth here,' I remarked to Catherine.

She pointed to part of the corn field. 'What is that man doing?'

I peered. A man was bending over planting a forked twig in the ground. When he had done that, he held up a little grey glove and a piece of cord.

'I shall ask,' I told her.

Riding over, I hailed him. 'Greetings stranger, may I ask what is it you're doing?'

The man grunted. 'I am about to hang a thief that is robbing me.'

'Where is this thief?' I enquired.

The man held up the grey glove and shook it.

'Pray tell me,' I was truly curious, 'what manner of thief is it that can fit into something as small as a glove?'

'It is a mouse. I caught it eating a sheaf of my corn that I had taken over to the barn.'

Catherine's face flushed. 'Is it fitting that a mighty farmer like yourself should demean himself so much as to hang a mouse?'

'I would hang all mice,' the man snarled, 'if they were gathered here now. Even if they were as large as cats, I would string them up. I hate them for eating food that is not theirs but mine. They do not work, till the land, yet they eagerly consume my daily toil.'

'Come now,' I reasoned. 'One mouse's appetite is not large. Let it go, man. Believe me, I am arguing for the sake of your own personal dignity.'

'My dignity will stay intact,' said the farmer. 'Justice must be done, thieves must be punished.'

62

Holding up the glove, he shook a little ball of fur into his open palm. He made a slip-knot which he put about the mouse's neck and moved towards the miniature gallows that he had erected.

'Stop!' I cried. 'I will give you three silver pieces if you spare the mouse and let it go free.'

'I will neither free it nor sell it,' replied the man.

Catherine looked at me accusingly. I felt somehow ridiculous, a knight of my calibre defending the honour of a mouse, but what alternative had I? I was about to halt the execution when I heard a jingle of harnesses and pounding of many hooves. Turning, I saw coming along the road a bishop in purple robes and behind him a whole retinue of serving-men, clerks and pack-horses.

'Greetings and blessing upon you all,' he said, lifting his hand as he passed by.

'This man,' I called out, 'is about to hang a mouse on the gallows for feeding on his corn.'

'Gracious!' exclaimed the bishop, stopping his train. 'Let me do a kindness to the paltry creature.' He looked hard at the farmer. 'I will offer you twenty silver pieces if you let it go.'

The man shook his head.

'I will give you seven pack horses and seven of my attendants,' said the bishop rashly.

The farmer was tenacious. 'I will take no price for this mouse. I have said I will hang it, and hang it I shall.'

'What right have you to hang it?' intervened Catherine. 'The creature may be innocent. How do you know it was this mouse at all?'

The farmer's face clenched with anger. 'I caught it in the act of eating my corn.'

'Is there a witness?' asked I.

'A witness!' the man roared. 'We are talking about a mouse.'

'Mice are God's creatures as well as men,' I pointed out, hoping to impress the bishop with my piety.

'I'm going to hang it,' said the farmer. 'You're all off your noddles.'

'Wait!' said the bishop. 'You cannot dole out rough justice in this manner. Not in a Christian land. As this good knight has pointed out, the mouse was also fashioned by the hand of God and has its rights. I see no alternative but to refer this matter to a special court set up for such matters. You, sir, will be the chief witness for the prosecution, and this knight, I suggest, who seems to have taken the cause of the mouse to heart, can act as the defendant, and let honour and justice prevail.'

All three of us, the farmer, Catherine and myself, were invited to ride along with the bishop's retinue. We agreed and jogged along in brooding silence. After about an hour, we reached a large monastery called Slingforth Abbey. In a field beyond the Lady Chapel was a decayed chapter-house where the local animal trials were held. Beasts, from rabbits to pigs and goats, had been tried, sentenced and spared in this building. The whole business merited mockery yet it had been elevated to law.

I waited with Catherine for several hours until various men came in and took their seats. The audience in the courtroom was made up mainly of farmers, who held grudges against various animals for devouring their crops or infecting their milk. I learnt that a stag had been gallowed the previous week for gnawing a field of swedes, and I realised that the case might be a close one.

The judge, clerk and jury were at last assembled. The clerk announced. 'My Lord, our next case is that of Farmer Tongs who accuses a certain mouse of eating his corn.'

A black-robed man with a saucer-shaped hat came in bearing the mouse in a cage. He set it down on a wooden table beside the bench. It was shivering in its mean little prison, and I could see Catherine flinch as she gazed upon it. The judge frowned at the mouse. 'Creature, do you plead guilty?'

A fragment of straw rustled and there was a scratching noise.

The clerk coughed. 'It looks as if the accused does not wish to commit himself.'

The judge shrugged. 'That is understandable. Well then, come on Farmer Tongs, take the stand. Let's hear what you've got to say.'

Father Tongs stood up grim-faced. Taking his place in the box, he glowered at the mouse. 'On the fourth Sunday after Lent', he declared, 'I entered my barn and found this mouse banqueting upon one of my sheaves of corn. I caught him in the act and put him in my glove, intending to hang him as thieves should hang. But I was thwarted and opposed by this knight and lady, who claimed that the issue was not clear-cut and that the mouse might be innocent.'

The judge leaned over and addressed the cage. 'What about the accused? Have you anything to say in mitigation?'

The mouse emitted three squeaks.

'See!' said Farmer Tongs quivering. 'The creature has owned to its guilt.'

'I cannot accept that as a confessioin,' replied the judge. 'We will now hear the case for the defence which is being conducted by Sir Galahad, a knight of some renown, I believe.'

Farmer Tongs moved out of the box, and I replaced him. Surveying the jurors, I tried to assess their characters. Solid, severe types, they seemed, not easily moved by eloquence. Yet having got so far, I had to put up a good showing.

'Gentlemen of the jury,' I began, nodding toward Farmer Tongs, 'at the heart of this case is a prosperous man. I have learned that he owns two farms, a herd of fifty cattle, ten horses, six serving wenches, one mill, sixteen pigs, thirty fowls, a duck and a pond. While this harvest mouse owns nothing, save for a tiny hole in the ground, which this proud farmer may well contest, for the hole is probably on his land. I ask you, gentleman, what is really the object of the prosecution's case. What is the crime this frail grey-coated creature is guilty of? Nibbling an ear of corn – an ear of corn! Good gentlemen, I ask you, what does the prosecution expect of a mouse? For the creature to say to itself: I cannot nibble this ear of corn, for it is not mine, and to eat any food that is not mine is wicked. Good gentlemen, mice do not think like that. They have not been brought up that way. They know nothing of human morality or etiquette or else they would not be mice. They are simply as God made them, and God made them to live in holes, eat corn, wash their whiskers, look after their young and not be judged by the alien laws of man. So, gentlemen of the jury, to condemn this mouse would not be like condemning a criminal. It would be condemning something for merely being itself. It would even be condemning God – after all He, in his wisdom, fashioned the mouse as such. This cannot be allowed. Besides, its logical extension enters the domain of idiocy. For instance, a rich man is sipping a goblet of rasberry wine, and when he puts it down, a wasp begins sipping from the goblet. The wasp is only being a wasp but judged by human laws it is also being a thief. You appreciate my point gentlemen of the jury: that if you do not find this mouse innocent, you must be prepared to try the whole animal and insect kingdom for obeying their innermost natures.'

I finished my speech. The jury was asked to retire and consider the verdict. I waited tense-lipped, glancing across to Catherie, who was sitting at the back of the court-room. She gave me a wave and a smile.

Only ten minutes later the jury trooped back. The judge asked, 'Have you reached your verdict?'

The head of jury stepped forward. 'We have my Lord.'

'And what is it?'

'We find the vermin guilty.'

Affronted, I clenched my fists and hissed out an angry breath. All my darts of logic and wit had glanced off their armour-plated minds. In fact, had I stated things more simply, I might have fared better: flowery rhetoric had been my downfall.

The clerk nodded and scratched with his quill. The judge addressed the cage. 'Mouse, you have been found guilty. Is there anything you would like to say?'

The mouse scampered and scratched.

'I hereby sentence you,' the judge intoned wearily, 'to be hung by the neck at the crossways. The execution shall take place in one hour. Farmer Tongs may attend but no one else.'

Cheering in the court. Clearly the farmers approved the verdict. The clerk draped a black cloth over the cage and proceeded to take it away.

'Not so fast,' said I, blocking his way. 'I will have that cage.'

'It is the property of the court!' the clerk protested.

'No so!' cried I.

I thrust my knee beneath the table at which he had been sitting and gave it a mighty kick. It toppled and crashed amid the seated jurors – fearing injury they scattered. Snatching up the cage, I made for the door. The farmers swept towards me, flint-eyed and furious, holding rakes, scythes and hoes. I threw the cage over their heads. Catherine fielded it and made a bolt for the door.

As the uncouth turnips bore down, I slashed my sword, cutting deadly arcs in the air. That held them at bay, until a few began lunging at me with their rude implements. A rake was thrust against my wrist forcing the sword from my hand. Cursing, I fought back using every low method: kneeing groins, biting ears and butting stomachs. As I struck a wedge through their massed bulk, I scattered seats and threw law books in their faces. They let out deep bovine groans and locked together in a knotted pack. I responded by vaulting over their bent bodies, using their backs as stepping-stones, and moving from fray to fray, until the confusion was so total that no one could make sense of it. Thus I was able to slip out and escape.

Catherine was outside holding the cage. Larkspur and her own horse were saddled and reined.

We galloped away together. When we had put the monastery several miles behind us, we dismounted and sat in the grass beside the track. Unhooking the cage from the saddle, I flicked open the door, and the tiny corn-gnawer scurried out, gave two distinct squeaks of gratitude, a whip of tail, and it lost itself among the tall spears of grass.

A tender mist veiled Catherine's eyes. 'Galahad, you are a noble knight,' said she, giving me a kiss.

And that is how I won a woman's heart with a mouse.

# 11

# THE BARROW GHOSTS

That evening, having released the mouse, we set up camp. We chose a place not far from the road, near a tall mound of earth called Wimble Toot. Beside it grew a gnarled and calloused yew. A silent place. No crows stirred, no cattle cropped, save for one elderly three-legged sheep who seemed to have a fondness for the place. When it was dark, we saw a light flitting around the base of the mound. It was coming from a fire which had recently been lit and I went over to take a look. Crouching over the flames was an elderly man with a stumpy body, accusing eyes, a pinched, brown face. He gripped a staff crowned with a lion carving. A big fat cat lay cradled in his lap. I recognised him straight away.

'Hello, Dylfric, remember me. I'm the young Galahad. From Dykesyat. My father was Court Baron. He built the chapel for you on Dorville's Hill.'

The anchorite sneezed. 'Ah yes, I remember you like the pestilence, Galahad. You would make faces at me while I prayed and tease me by eating great slabs of bread and cheese, just five feet from my fasting-chair.'

'Boys will be boys,' said I.

'Your father was a good man. Is he still alive?'

I nodded. 'Still doleing out justice to the oppressed?

'And what of you? You have become a knight, I hear.'

'Yes. I'm presently occupied looking for the Grail.'

Dylfric sniffed. 'Very laudable no doubt. But I think you'll have to become a good deal holier if you want to lay your hands on that.'

'My problem is,' I explained, 'that I find it difficult to sustain a pious mood for more than an hour. Can you recommend anything?'

The anchorite brought out a little bag and undid the cord at the top. 'Here,' he said, taking out a small glass phial, 'is a speck of blood from the blessed martyr, St Lubricious, and that should assist any such problems.'

'How much?'

'The blood is one shilling, five coppers the phial.'

'Do you possess anything cheaper?'

'Cheaper!' he exclaimed. 'I'm trying to save your immortal soul. If you want salvation, you must pay the going rate.'

At this point Catherine – unbeknown she had followed me – intervened. She strode between us, cheeks aflame, cloak swirling proudly. 'I do not agree with the sale of relics and indulgences,' she said. 'Either a man sets an example by his life, or else he is not worthy. You cannot purchase goodness.'

At the sight of her slender form, Dylfric hunched into a tight ball of resentment. 'Get thee hence me, Satan!' he snarled. 'Let me not be tempted!'

Flinging himself on the ground, he began thumping the dust, foam flowering from his jaws. He drummed his forehead against the earth, imploring, 'Lord give me strength to resist – give me strength to resist!'

'Calm down, Dylfric,' said I. 'Every time you meet a girl, must you go through all this writhing and rolling? Why don't you just say something pleasant like – Morning ma'am, that's a pretty dress you're wearing.'

Dylfric stood up and dusted himself down. 'Galahad,' he replied with dishevelled dignity, 'you force me to reiterate the most basic points. If temptation presents no particular problem, then one has achieved nothing by overcoming it. Hence, if one seriously wishes to pursue religion as a career, one must emphasise the spiritual struggle aspect.'

'Is your career blossoming?' I asked.

'I'm off to see Henry, Prior of the cathedral monastery at Ducklehurst,' he replied. 'The place is infested with a fury of mice and rats, and so I thought I'd take Black Susan with me.' He gave the big fat cat a few quick strokes.

'We are but five miles from Ducklehurst? Why are you resting here?'

'A conclave of monks invited me to spend the night on the tall mound yonder. They say it is haunted by certain unhealthy spirits, and asked me to perform the ritual of banishment.'

'Can you enter the tomb?'

Dylfric nodded. 'Yes, it is filled with pottery, shells and bones and has an evil smell about it.'

'What will you do when you confront these ghosts?'

'I will ask them, in the name of the Father, Son and Holy Ghost, to leave the tomb and cease to haunt the living.'

'Well, good luck,' said I. 'We will see you on the morrow and learn of your progress.'

The next morning, I was having breakfast with Catherine when Dylfric appeared. He stood above the campfire, shivering, envious at the speckled trout we were grilling. As his nose savoured the dusky fumes, his restless eyes scanned the heavens.

I asked, 'Did you exorcise the unhealthy spirits?'

'Nay Galahad,' he replied frowning. 'They are most vengeful and stubborn ghouls. When I took out my Bible and read the appropriate text, a big black dog appeared and ran around me barking like a fiend. Next a pile of bones came alive under my nose, and a tall, thin, hot-eyed man with red lips and boils on his face, began to leer and mouth obscenities in my ear. Then a third figure blew into the tomb, clad in a white robe with a hood, like a priest of that infernal religion the Romans supposedly stamped out. All three of them traipsed around me, mocking my prayers and exhortations, making foul mists steam up before my eyes. I tested them with every exorcism I knew, but they would not go, and eventually I had to give up and leave the tomb.'

I gestured him to take a place beside the fire. 'Sit down and have some grilled fish, Dylfric. Are you sure you witnessed all this? These ghosts, you know, may be the result of praying too hard on an empty stomach.'

'If you doubt my words, Galahad, spend the night in the tomb yourself.'

'How shall I get to see these spirits?'

'In the middle of the night, you will hear a knocking on the walls, like a shower of giant hailstones. And then the dog will come in and bark at you. Next a red-faced lustful man will taunt you, who shall be followed by the pagan priest who will boast of terrible rites.'

'Do you desire the company of ghosts?' asked Catherine.

'I've nothing against new acquaintances,' said I.

'Perhaps one should not converse with dead things.'

'We must proceed one leg at a time, as lawyers go to heaven.'

Catherine asked, 'You have no fear?'

I shrugged. 'I fear the living more than the dead. They have more to gain and lose.'

'You are a mocker, Galahad. You should wear a cap and bells.'

'Cap and bells, habit and tonsure, crown and sceptre – different hats, different ways of jesting!'

'You admit no difference, Galahad,' Catherine gave a look of disapproval, 'between people and their callings. And yet, in order to do good by anyone, you need to fix such things clearly! You cannot treat all the same. I think you turn life into a pageant of escapades and revels, so that you can slip out of things with greater ease.'

'We may learn answers to such matters,' said I, 'for we are about to converse with the shades.'

'What if this place is truly evil?' she asked playfully, yet with an underlying disquiet. 'Galahad, remember what happened to St Catcott? He slept in a pagan tomb and was attacked by horned creatures in the night. He was taken up into the freezing air, dropped down to earth, stripped naked, beaten with sticks and almost died of fever.'

'That is his story,' said I, 'and he has prospered from it. I heard him preach once in the chapel at Camelot. He sprayed us with spittle and hellfire until our brains were riddled.'

She gave me an admonishing glance. 'He had been attacked by dangerous spirits and sought to warn others.'

Realising she was serious, I placed a hand on her shoulder and her expression calmed. Though I hid it, I was frightened, too. But I reasoned that, allowing for so many living physical antagonists, possessed of clubs and swords with which they will assail you, only an obsessed, problem-seeking nature would seek out such a gang in the invisible world. Certainly I was not going to be lured into such apprehensions, not in the wake of such a mild, kindly day, full of the moisture and balm of early summer. After a bright morning, we had bidden farewell to Dylfric and saddled his horse, then watched him and Black Susan trot along the eastern track to Ducklehurst. The afternoon we had spent riding and fishing, and now, in the early evening, drawn by some morbid compulsion, Catherine and I trudged towards the barrow, half-fearful, half-curious, but determined to find out what, if anything, did haunt the tomb.

It was a long chambered barrow with an entrance of upright slabs and a capstone padded around with turf. We entered and gazed at the minimal furnishings. On the floor was a crouched skeleton with a circle of seashells strewn around his feet and a broken ale-jar and a few bronze pins. There was also a little exorcism bell left by Dylfric who believed that the most horrid spirits and malevolent demons would be mightily afeared by the noise of a little silver clapper. Catherine and I sat on the hard earth floor and looked at each other.

'We can do nothing but wait,' said I.

Catherine nodded. To pass the hours, we played at dice with small rounded pebbles until the sun went down. The last red rays narrowed, flashed fiercely, and then edged down behind the dark clump of trees. The tomb became cold, lightless and the smell of dried decay sharpened in our nostrils. Indeed, then it seemed a most gloomy sepulchre, steeped in the essences and aromas of the past. Shivering, Catherine lit a candle and drew her knees up clasping them with her arms.

'We are having exciting adventures, Galahad,' she said with a smile. 'Meeting ghosts before our time.'

'Have some wine,' said I, offering her my pitcher.

She shook her head. 'You drink too much wine, Galahad. You have it with everything. It is your shield against the world.'

'Did you know,' said I, 'that the streams of Heaven consist of flowing rivulets of red and white wine? It is of so light and delicious a flavour that, when the angels drink it, they float up in the air without flexing their wings.'

Catherine observed tartly. 'You mock religion one moment and then shelter your indulgence under it.'

'Drinking is no indulgence. Vines are the pillars that hold up this crumbling world.'

What am I saying, I thought? I was starting to drone like Hugh Meadmore, prolonged contact with whom at Camelot had indeed increased my capacity for consumption. I must moderate my way or else I'd find not the Grail but the less glorious spectre of an angry taverner demanding further payment.

My voice faded. Catherine gave a little shudder. A shower of hail, or small stones, peppered the roof of the tomb. I held my breath and put my arm around Catherine. The candle guttered. An icy wind frisked through the open entrance and made a hissing sound as it nosed among the shells and stones.

A deep muffled bark came from outside.

'Spirit or demon!' I called, springing to my feet. 'My name is Galahad. I am a knight of Arthur's court. Make yourself known to me. Let there be commerce between us.'

I waited with arms and legs of stone. Catherine's pupils dilated and her shoulders shook. Another bark and a scraping, shuffling noise. Then an immense grey dog like a four-legged hedge strode in the tomb, sniffed and cocked its leg against the stone arch. A plume of mist floated up from the spot he had anointed.

'I am a big black dog,' the creature announced in a gruff bass. 'But I am also a ghost. I am the guardian of the barrow and frighten away simple folk. Woof, woof, I go, and they run away – what is the precise meaning of this noise? Does it announce presence or seek to dispel it? I say this as one interested in words, their shades and connotations. But I cannot take such things further. You see, I have no friends here, save for the three-legged sheep who says baah and aah to whatever observations I happen to make.'

When I had recovered from the shock, I breathed out harshly, wondering what on earth to do. The fluency of the animal's delivery and the dignity of its bearing was remarkable. I could not help warming to creature. Yes, 'warming' *was* the right word. For even the dog's ghostly black fur called up deep-buried coals lodged in slumbering hillsides and caverns. Not the dumb black of death but a singing black that, once heated, produced a dish of flame that purred and crackled with content. No fanged hunting-hound – no, it belonged to that steadfast, comforting breed, tall and shaggy, yet bravely buoyant in water, with furry fans spreading around the paws, a broad benevolent brow and a gaze of such benignity that one could not think of it as a dog, so much as a kind, wise friend, who would stand by one through all the vicissitudes and disavowals the world might bring.

'You look sturdy and well-groomed,' I observed, 'despite your present status.'

'My old master,' the dog mused, 'used to take me running in the hills. Chase the clouds, my faithful hound, he would say, chase the clouds!'

'Inspiring,' said I, 'inspiring but impossible.'

'Ah, that is the purpose of inspiration,' the dog rejoined, 'to stretch attainment beyond ordinary bounds.'

Noticing that he still wore a collar, I leaned over and read. 'Sir Peregrine Montacutus – do you remember him?'

The dog barked affirmatively. 'Yes, Sir Peregrine was my old master, late of Blackwell Manor. He lies in the old church beyond the mill. You cannot miss him. He reclines on the altar tomb, clad in stone armour with a sheathed sword hanging from his jewelled belt. Not long after he left England to join a crusade, I died – a dog's years seldom exceed those of his master. A year later Sir Peregrine was stricken with the falling sickness. He was taken bad at the gates of Antioch and saw little fighting. When they brought back his body to Blackwell, his wife Lady Sarah put up almshouses in his memory and every day visited his tomb until she herself passed on and was placed beside him. Above his head is a painted shield on which are carved the symbols of death: scythe, cut grass, a skull and hourglass. That faithful hound on whom his feet rests is me.'

'Thank you, dog, for your informative speech,' said I. 'Perhaps you may care to enlighten us on the nature of the otherworld. Do you enjoy being a ghost?'

The dog shrugged and swished its tail. 'It is, you may say, satisfactory. But there is a missing feel to it. There are bones for eating but they lack the scrunchy flavour of living bones.'

Catherine expressed her sympathy. The dog wrinkled its nose.

'Smells also lack piquance,' he grumbled. 'When I was alive, the earth was most odiferous – if you'll excuse my use of an epithet that may seem pretentious. I would water a tree or wayside cross, stop, sniff, move on, water something else, maybe a whipping-post or a gilt shrine, and then stop and sniff again. What a cheerful young pup I was! Leg a-cock, I was ready to take on the world! Ambition I had in plenty: I desired to sniff the hindparts of King Cedric's hunting bitch. But now I am a ghost, all my fun is finished. I sniff the thin vapours of the otherworld, gnaw the bone of despair, and squirt jets of twinkly mist 'gainst the pallid shanks of wraiths and phantoms.'

'You have spoken well, dog,' said I. 'Your eloquence and posture are a credit to your species. You have provided me with fine insights into the nature of the beyond.'

'Think nothing of it, my good fellow,' replied the black dog, and, cocking his leg against the crouched skeleton, released another puff of mist.

The swirl of silvery vapour clung to the skeleton. Gradually it took on a dense meshed texture, obscuring the fretwork of bones, wrapping like a riding-cloak around the arms and legs. We watched this process until none of the skeleton was visible. We were looking at the wavering outline of a body without a face. Then the shafts of the limbs glowed dirty white and filled out and hardened. A patch of red-plush skin appeared on the crown of the skull; small copper hairs shot up in wiry tufts. The hunched-up body began to stir very slightly. Life flickered in the eyes which glowed amber then gold. Slowly the bony chin lifted from the rib-cage. Catherine's mouth dropped open and I braced myself for another encounter.

We were gaping at a tall, thin man, with a pointed head, owl's eyes and a complexion that was disfigured by boils.

'And who be you, ghost?' asked I.

'I am Orderic,' the man answered, 'formerly steward of Lord Bec of Toskington Manor. I am thoroughly tired of being a ghost.'

'Why is that?'

The man sighed. 'For months you wait around longing for a friendly face, a glass of good ale, a chunk of barley cake, or the touch of leather against the skin. But all that's left is this sensation of lightness, which I find most alien to my nature. You are more fragile than a gust.'

The steward blew through his mouth to demonstrate his point. Icy needling breezes stirred the stagnant air.

'Cease that immediately!' I snapped. ''Tis like conversing with a pair of bellows.'

'The mightiest bellows,' said the steward, 'could not cool my ardour when I was alive. For I was hot, lewd and lusty. I took many a maid in the cellars and barns of my lord and master. But now, although I am still bloated with desire, I can do naught to satisfy it. Last night, I was blown into the bedchamber of a most beautiful lady and watched her remove her clothes. I saw her skirts slide over her knees and her bodice fall to the floor. I was sizzling like a powder-keg, but I had no proper body, and all my roused-up frustration could do was make a curtain rustle.'

'I am sorry to hear of your problems,' said I. 'But did you honestly expect the afterlife to be a bawdy-house for the likes of you?'

'Woof!' agreed the dog. 'Yes, what did you expect, steward? To be tumbling skeletons in their shrouds?'

'How did you both die?'

'I got old and rheumy-eyed,' replied the dog, 'and caught the distemper.'

'My wife,' said the steward, 'threw me out of a third floor window. She had spied on me while I was tumbling a comely wench called Mary.'

'Did she work in the dairy?' asked the black dog.

'Nay, but she was very hairy.' The steward grinned.

'Less of that smirking lewdness,' said I. 'A lady is present.'

I nodded towards Catherine. Her hands were struggling with the edge of her skirt which was flapping above her knees. The whites of her thighs gleamed beneath the mutinous hem. I shouted at the steward. 'Stop that at once!'

Orderic's eyes dulled from gold to amber. The skirts settled in place like tired wavelets and Catherine smoothed them out. Orderic, still in his crouching posture, gazed glumly down at his feet which had not properly materialised and remained dense misty blobs.

'And there is another one of you I believe.'

The dog yawned. 'The Druid, yes, he will turn up, if you ring the bell.'

I rang the bell. A light rattling noise, like shaken bones and beads, followed by a dull shriek. A hunched figure stepped into the tomb, a malevolent dwarf of a man with a scarred and scornful face and absent slatey eyes that seemed sunk in the slough of some past resentment. He was hooded and cloaked and his robe had sprigs of mistletoe pinned to it. A bone-belt was wrapped around his waist, and in his left hand he clutched a tiny grey skull, which may have belonged to a child.

'Welcome,' said I. 'We have not been introduced.'

The Druid lifted his head and spoke wearily. 'My name is Lyr Indractes. I was born and tutored on the island of Anglesey. I was a Druid. There we had set up many shrines and altars, adorned with fresh-cut heads, hearts, entrails, dead ravens and the jaws of giant pikes. We thought them nice but the Romans resented our decoration and our influence. Suetonius was ordered to wipe out the priesthood. Flying the windsocks of war, the legion marched to Anglesey, and we drew up our ranks to oppose them. As the cavalry bore down, summoning up the spirits of the dead, we hurled curses at them. Our black-clad woman ran among the soldiery lashing flaming brands and howling. But their swords hacked the sinews of our unprotected necks. We died with hatred boiling in our throats. And now I am a ghost, adrift in the air like pollen, bored and vengeful.'

'There is no solace in your condition,' I asked.

'There is no solace in death,' replied the Druid. 'Yet, what meaning was there in life? Years I spent skull-collecting to make our shrines seem tasteful to the eye. We had enough bones to build an ivory palace...' He sighed and fluttered an empty hand. 'All of no account. They are gone, crumbled away, like the ashes of ancient feasts.'

'Decomposition is no bad thing,' I pointed out. 'It makes the world a tidier place.'

My remark failed to lighten his spirits. 'I am no longer learned,' he complained. 'I have forgotten it all. Once I was versed in astronomy, mathematics and botany. I could name all the plants: belladonna, chickweed, fennel, henbane, sorrel, alkanet, samphire, bedstraw...'

The black dog gave a gruff bark. 'That is enough, Druid. We get tired of you and your lists of flowers.'

'We get tired of everything,' echoed Orderic the steward. 'O how blissful it would be to go out like a light!'

'The anchorite Dylfric,' said I, 'tried to banish you. He told me you treated him most uncivilly.'

'That man,' the black dog groaned, 'was exceedingly tiresome. He brought out this little black book and pelted us with a misery of holy phrases. So we fought back and put the chillies on him.'

'Yes,' agreed the steward. 'He fumed about the sins of the flesh so loudly that I almost shrieked with desire.'

'He called me Satan's cur,' added the dog. 'And I a good Christian hound.'

'He called me a heathen,' muttered the Druid. 'And I only I showed him this nice skull my grandad had given me.'

A long pause. The three ghosts stared at Catherine and I with forlorn expectancy. Eventually I was moved to ask, 'What can we do to help you?'

'I ask for nothing,' said the dog. 'But if you light a fire in this tomb and burn a little meat over it, the flavour will transport me to another realm, and I will no longer haunt the earth.'

'When I was young,' explained the Druid, 'my sister would sing to me the popular air *My Dear Old Headhunting Mama*. If only I could hear that sweet strain once more, I would happily drift away to Hell, Hades, Tir-an-Og, Anglesey or Avalon.'

'I know that song well,' said the dog. 'You should have consulted me on this matter before, Druid. *My Dear Old Headhunting Mama* was one of the first musical pieces I ever became proficient at. I learnt it off an Irish tinker when I was a mere puppy.'

'If you want to see the end of me,' said Orderic the steward, 'I must implore this kind lady here,' he nodded at Catherine, 'to slip off the garment she is wearing. The sight of her with nothing on will make me so hot that I will flare up like a wisp of gas and never be seen again.'

I looked at Catherine. She was staring round-eyed but did not contradict any of the suggestions. So I turned to the ghosts, saying. 'We will help all three of you on your way. Which of you would like to go first?'

The Druid stepped forward, fingering the little grey skull.

'We will need your singing voice,' I told the black dog, 'if we are to help the Druid extinguish himself.'

'Fine,' barked the dog. 'Have you got a flute handy? I prefer singing to an accompaniment.'

I glanced at Catherine. She searched in her travelling bag and took out her flute. Raising it to her lips, she let out a few practise notes. The dog gave an approving bark and waddled over. I patted its shaggy hide which felt like a hairy mist. Lifting its head, the dog began to howl the sentimental strains of *My Dear Old Headhunting Mama*. Catherine joined in with the flute, and they made a fine duo, her and the ghost-dog, who was obviously a sensitive and talented musician, despite his unartistic appearance. On hearing it, the Druid's eyes dimmed and a tear slid over his cheek. Quickly he thinned and faded away like chalk in rain, leaving a cloak behind with a few dried pods of mistletoe pinned to it.

'Well done, dog,' said I. 'You can do a fine obliggato.'

'Pray do not burden me with compliments,' the dog replied. 'Heat up a piece of meat and let me be drawn up in an aromatic cloud.'

'I have no meat, only fish.'

The dog nodded. 'Meat, fish, it is no matter, so long as the smell is good and strong.'

Lighting a fire, I selected a trout, slapped it in a dish of flour, added herbs and put a skewer through it. Then Catherine took over, holding it above the fire. As the scented flames flickered, the shaggy ghost-dog came forward, lolled out its large red tongue and began to howl. Delicious fumes pierced the air as the trout's scales curled and shrivelled leaving pale flesh. The dog took a deep sniff, and I stroked it. The fur crackled like dry straw. Slowly it grew transparent, and then it seemed to draw up into the fire like a column of grey-black smoke. Now there was only myself, Catherine and the ghost of the lusty steward left.

Catherine looked distressed. 'Must I go through this?'

'If you desire to give an unhappy ghost rest,' said the steward.

Catherine looked at me sternly. 'Galahad, turn your back.'

I put my back to the fire and waited. There was a swish, a silken rustle, a slithering of silk over knees, and I heard a little gasp of joy, followed by a flash of light. Turning, I glimpsed Catherine's naked body, all lustrous and lily-smooth, with the two hot gold-rimmed pupils of the steward lingering like tiny lanterns in the grey air of the tomb. They went out in a blink to be replaced by mine, gazing upon Catherine crouched there, with an expression of stern modesty, yet nothing else on.

She bent down to retrieve her garments. But I stepped forward and took her by the hand, saying. 'Do not cover yourself. We only enjoy the sun when the clouds are cleared.'

Lowering my head, I began to kiss her breasts. The next moment her knee came up and struck me somewhere, and I rolled around groaning. By the time the pain had cleared, she had already left the tomb. Sadly I took up my pitcher of wine and began to follow her down to the horses.

But I was pulled back by loud bark. I re-entered the tomb where a triangular patch of black mist was floating above the embers. Two glossy-brown eyes shone through like conkers. The head of the black dog stared at me. It opened it jaws, unfurling a steaming tongue which flicked up and slapped against its nose.

'Before I curl up in the kennels of eternity, knight, a word of thanks and some advice. The way of the Grail is in the wild lands of the north. Take that direction by way of the Forest of Wandlebury. There you will meet Herne the Hunter, the stag-god of the woods, and gain information and a companion on the way. Tread warily – Vikings will waylay you and payments will have to be made.'

'Will I find the Grail?'

The question was left hanging, for the dog instantly departed.

# 12

# HERNE THE HUNTER

S ir Hugh Meadmore groaned. Gradually his head lolled forward and bathed its brow in the small puddle of ale that he had lately spilt on the inn table.

'I am not a knight, Galahad,' he confided gravely. 'Faith, I am a galloping disgrace! I do not know why you waste your time talking to me.'

I did not know either. In fact, I would have been gladly relieved of Meadmore's company. But after taking Catherine to her relatives, well-heeled Cirencester wool-magnates, I felt a gnawing sorrow. To know someone, grow attached, then set them down for the sake of a quest whose culmination is as likely to bring sorrow as happiness is a strange thing. Is it because we place duty above happiness? Or is it because one is frightened to risk living for one's own pleasure? For if one fails, where can one turn? Farewell! A strange word imprinted with the chill of sadness. For it carries the possibility of 'not faring well' – of riding out to an unnamed destiny beyond the reaches of former friendship. Ah – how we spurn our deepest feelings in case they may destroy us! Yes, with Catherine gone, I lost my way. I desired respite from galloping and Grail-searching. A coarse yearning overcame me for tavern life and bawdy houses. So I stopped and put up at a wayside inn called the Disgraced Deacon, four miles outside Cambridge. There I was greeted by this armoured failure, who babbled incoherently, his moods varying between unctious flattery and personal criticism.

'Galahad, are you listening. I am at my wit's end. I was telling you what a failure I am. Do you know what Arthur called me? A chivalric disaster!'

'Do not be so despondent, Meadmore,' I answered, despite my inner rage. 'Try a little willpower. You might find your old fighting self again. Cut down on the wine and make an effort to help someone. A maiden in distress perhaps.'

'A maiden in distress. In distress. Faith Galahad, I am in despair. I am a drunk, and what is worse is that I am happy as a drunk. I like drinking. Do you understand that, Galahad?'

I shrugged. 'Clearly you have achieved your ambition.'

'No, I was lying then, Galahad. I despise myself, truly I do. Look at you. A fine man – the peerless flower of all knighthood, that's what I heard someone call you. A peerless flower.'

'Meadmore, you must not flatter me. I am not a girl.'

'Nonsense, you deserve flattery, Galahad. Why, I've heard you're on some great quest – searching for the Holy Grail. The Holy Grail! Faith, I cannot even find my rere-braces in the morning.'

'You overpraise my paltry efforts, Meadmore. I have many failings.'

'Nonsense Galahad. You have no failings, while I am nothing but failings. I am all wind and water. Why, compared with me, the lowliest maggot is an uncrowned king.'

'Do not be too hard on yourself. All knights like a drink.'

Silence for a while and then Meadmore's head slumped forward and struck the table. 'I have to be getting back,' he groaned. 'Yes, I must leave and return to my wife.' He forced himself up and blinked at me. 'Faith, I forgot – I have no wife any longer. She left me years ago. I do not blame her. I would leave myself were it possible. My life is worthless, Galahad.'

'It is not worthless,' said I, 'but it is of no great use to anyone at the present.'

I went over and hauled him him up, edging him step by step towards the tavern door. Seeing he was being enticed to leave, he grew sulky and rebellious. He began to struggle and heave in protest, and I tightened my hold. 'Let go of me, man!' he cried. 'Do you think I have not yet learned to walk? Why, I am the finest knight in all Christendom, a peerless flower, the best tilter and jouster that ever rode forth.'

Outside dark clouds cloaked the rainy sky. It proved an immense struggle to get Meadmore on his horse and slot his feet into the stirrups. Once astride, he looked down blearily at me, saying. 'Did you know, Galahad, that this drinking is a mere passing fancy? I will show the world the metal of which I'm made.'

'That's the spirit, Meadmore.'

'You see, Galahad,' he prattled. 'I have nothing against you. Truly you are a courteous fellow, but as a knight you are useless, nothing. Why, I have watched your swordplay. Frankly it is childish – you move your feet like a French dancing-master. I could make you yield in ten seconds.'

I felt like yielding at that very moment, feeling bored, wet and oppressed. Leading Meadmore's horse away, I set it on the right path, slapped its rump, and it broke into a trot, bearing its disputatious and dissolute burden over the plain towards whatever haphazard destiny awaited it.

I went back to the tavern. 'Landlady, what's the bill?' I asked.

Taking out a piece of slate marked with charcoal, she read off the figures.

'You've had two shillings worth of wine.'

'Yes, that's true.'

'Bread, four coppers. Pork and eels, six coppers.'

'I nodded. 'Correct.'

'A girl, one shilling.'

'Yes, I do remember.'

'Hay for your horse, two coppers.'

'Faith! That horse will be the ruin of me.'

Before me stretched the broak oak forest of Wandlebury, which the ghost dog had directed me to explore, a seething hive of wolves, serpents and fallow deer. It was a sacred place, where ancient gods were alleged to dwell, where the Wild Huntsman galloped with his demon horde, and where Herne the Hunter, the horned god of the oak-tree, dwelt and dispensed wisdom to truth-seekers.

After riding for several hours, I came to a clearing in the forest. A youth with curly gold hair, wearing a tunic of green brocaded silk and boots of new cordwain, was sitting upon the stump of a tree chattering to himself. He greeted me with a smile. I halted Larkspur and went over to converse with him, telling him I was from Arthur's court and seeking the Grail.

'I will instruct how to find what you are seeking,' he told me. 'Sleep here tonight, and rise early and take the road that goes through the valley. You will come to a mound in the middle of a clearing, and beside that mound is a fountain with a silver bowl and a marble slab. You are to scoop up some water, and throw some over the slab, and then you will hear a great peal of thunder – you will think heaven and earth are shaking. After the peal, there will come a cold shower of hailstones, which will sting your face.'

The youth paused, gazed up solemnly at the sky, and continued. 'Thereafter a flight of birds shall alight on a nearby tree and begin singing a sweet and delightful song. Even while you are enraptured by it, you shall hear the sound of panting and groaning. Thereupon you shall see a knight on a pure black horse with a pennon of pure black bliant upon his spear. And he will fall upon you briskly, and if you flee before him, he will overtake you, but if you do not move, he will leave you unharmed.'

As I listened, fascinated by this swiftly unfolding narrrative, a man rode into the clearing, a elderly fellow upon a piebald horse. He climbed off and came over, taking me aside and whispering, 'I suppose he has been telling you that story about about the fountain and the black knight. Poor boy, he has lost his wits, and he is always bothering strangers with fantastic yarns. I beg your indulgence, sir, but he is rather immature.'

'If you follow this black knight,' the youth went on, 'he will lead you to this castle which is painted all over black and green, flying pennons adorned with eagles and doves. In this castle there is a chapel, and upon the altar within you will find a cross all studded with rubies and beryls. If you take up the cross and knock it thrice against the wall, a tiny black man will appear bearing a cup of brass in one hand and a cup of wood in the other.'

'You see,' said the old man, with tears in his eyes. 'He is quite mad, my only son. Yes, sir knight, I took him to a doctor who diagnosed the malady. It is the jabberick humours, he said, steaming from his kidneys up the windpipe, and finally inflaming the brain and bringing on a fable-telling frenzy. Have pity! He cannot help it – this awful spouting of legend and lore!'

'Is there no cure?' I asked.

'There is none,' he replied, 'unless you sit around me all day and listen to him and grow grey hairs like me.'

'This black man,' the youth purled like a stream, 'will offer you to drink from both cups, and, if you should choose the one that is wood, a gigantic swan will swoop above you with an amber chain around its neck. But if you should drink out of the brass cup, a lion will charge forth, all royally arrayed in scarlet and purple. He will let out a mighty roar, whereupon…'

'I mean, what would you do, sir knight,' the old fellow asked, 'if you had a son who spoke to you like that? I keep telling him to take a good, sound job in a piggery or stable but no! All he does is ramble around yarning to any hawker or commoner with the patience to listen?'

'Come man, cheer up!' said I. 'His malady has made him more interesting than many a saner fellow. Give him a quill and parchment, and he may in the end become as famous as Caedmon.'

'You are very considerate, sir knight. Thank you for your advice.'

Before I left the clearing, I gave the boy as a gift my small knife with a walrus-bone handle. He stared at it, smiled and therewith embarked upon another long story. But I was already astride Larkspur and galloping out of the clearing and down into the valley.

I skirted the banks of the stream, climbed above it and entered the woods again. This was the deepest and most unvisited part of the great forest. The trees were wide-boughed, lofty as towers, and the greenness enclosed one like a shawl. Splashing through a stream and over a bank of purple flowers, I trotted into a clearing, where I experienced a shock. A marble slab had been set beside the mouth of a fountain, and there was a silver bowl chained to it – exactly as the youth had described! I dismounted, tethered Larkspur and dabbled my hand in the seething clear liquid. With a twinge of curiosity, I did as the boy had recommended: scooping up the water and slinging it over the marble slab.

It did not start raining, no birds or black knight appeared, but I did hear a mighty panting and groaning.

Into the glade marched the figure of Herne the Hunter.

Report had come to me of his awesome appearance which I had dismissed as exaggerated. But I must confess to a passing shudder as this horned creature confronted me. On that gloomy afternoon, he seemed half-man, half-vegetation, with luminous green skin, strong triangular face and profuse beard of shrubby lichen. Heavy chains wreathed his shoulders and in his right hand was a huge iron club. Armlets and anklets of bark encased his wrists and calves which were thigh-thick right down to his enormous callussed feet! Most disturbing were his eyes: fire-red slits that glinted beneath huge shaggy antlers. They seemed to burn with an obscure inner-directed rage.

He let out another panting sound, whereupon a stag appeared. Herne raised his club and struck the earth, creating a punchbow in the soil. In response the stag let out of mighty belling, and in answer a host of animals appeared, rabbits, snakes, badgers, deer and small sleek-furred rodents. They edged towards me in the clearing, and I felt uneasy at this most unusual audience, so many bright inscrutable eyes staring.

Herne said. 'Dost thou see, little man, the power I have over these animals?'

'I am not here to dispute your popularity, Herne,' said I. 'I am Galahad from Arthur's court and am searching for the Holy Grail.'

Herne slowly lowered his iron club, whereupon the animals retreated back into the forest. 'The Grail,' he replied, 'that infernal cup! What use will it be? I should think there are drinking vessels enough at Camelot. Why, the other day, I saw a ale-flushed knight wandering in this forest. He was singing and shouting and tried to joust with a tree.'

'That man's name was Hugh Meadmore,' I told him. 'He is not a knight of sterling quality.'

'He was unable to unseat the giant oak.'

I laughed gently at this. Herne gave a nod of dour satisfaction. Clearly he liked to try his wit on a human audience.

'I hear you are a master of magic, Herne.'

'Magic!' Herne cried, shaking the chains around his shoulders. As he roared the word, a roll of thunder crashed through the trees. A tense silence. Then, with soft, fat plashes, rain began to fall, leaking into my armour and making the leaves glisten and droop.

'Your control of natural phenomena is remarkable,' I told him.

At this compliment Herne forced his lips into a sickly grin. Straightway the clouds were drawn up and dissolved. The sun appeared in a cerise sky; hot shafts spangled and laquered countless leaves. Woodpigeons began flitting and calling. A tiny red squirrel with an acorn in its paws hopped past my boots.

'You see,' groaned Herne, twisting his mouth in a regretful curl. 'I only have to make a face, express a certain mood, and nature plays the sedulous ape to my temperament. Can you imagine anything more tiresome?'

I could: Sir Hugh Meadmore. But I held my peace.

'I have all the elements under my command,' Herne went on. 'But I cannot admit to being fulfilled. I cannot die – it is not permitted – and am condemned to spend all my days in this forest. Mortals may sympathise, but what can they know of the interminable boredom of being guardian of all these trees? My days are spent patrolling uncommunicative oaks with this monstrous pair of horns grafted onto my forehead, which, believe me, are ill-fitting and none-too-comfortable. My companions are stags, badgers, spiders, squirrels, wolves, and of course the birds, whose ceaseless and foolish twitterings give me a headache. Aeons will pass, centuries of leaves pile up, decay, a thousand summers will broaden the boughs, and I will still be here, clanking these melodramatic chains, scaring a traveller or two – if the truth were known, I'd far prefer to sit and sup and exchange an intelligent word with him. No, sir knight, my life is not fulfilled, yet it will never alter or change. Not until this forest is cut down, and then my function will cease, and I will fade out like a will o' wisp. And what, I ask myself, will future generations remark of Herne? Ah Herne, they will say, he was a creature of habit, forest-bound, frightful to behold, able to control animals and the weather, but basically he did very little and left no one a jot happier.'

I pointed out. 'Herne, you express dissatisfaction with your work, which I grant has its monotonous aspects. But frankly, I think you should adopt a more manly attitude to your vocation. Take me as an example. I've been searching for the Grail for over a year, and that is by no means a May Day revel.'

'You can enjoy a far greater freedom than I,' argued Herne. 'I have inherited my role. While you, if you so desired, could abandon your quest and become a monk.'

'Heaven forbid!' said I. 'Monks wear habits of coarse woollen cloth. They hold skin-care unimportant and wash in cold water.'

Herne grimaced. 'Enough of this levity, knight! I find more wit in a corpse.'

'Your disposition is melancholic,' said I. 'You should smile more and whistle under adversity.'

Herne lowered his massive horns in weariness. 'I am tired of trees,' he said. 'Harmless things, they do much good, provide wood for fires and shelter for beasts and insects, but they are bound to an oath of silence. They do not speak, only rustle when the wind visits them, and how am I going to sharpen my wits on that?'

'Out there,' I gestured vaguely to the great without, 'you will not find an excess of wit and wisdom.'

'Pray, do not remind me,' said Herne. 'I realise that out there is a monotony of voices, just as here there is a monotony of rustlings. But it is a change of sound that

I seek, a different range of vocal inflections, a chord of music, the lilt of laughter, the clang of a blacksmith's anvil.'

I gazed at him, unwilling to be drawn into the net of sadness, which appeared to be his personal legacy. Then his eyes gleamed like molten coins, and he cocked his ear to one side, hearing a commotion in the undergrowth. A noise of snorting and grunting, and Sir Hugh Meadmore, performing his wild boar act, entered the clearing, nose to the ground as if probing for truffles. He crawled up to me on all fours and began sniffing at my boots.

'Get up Meadmore!' I ordered. 'You are pushing things to the limit of my endurance.'

Meadmore rose shakily to his feet, and then, seeing my companion, a naive enthusiasm crept into his eye. 'My - you're Herne the Hunter!' he exclaimed. 'My grandmother used to tell me about you. She said you banqueted every day on chestnuts and acorns and always left out some for the squirrels. Is that true? By Jupiter, look at those horns! They must be thirty-pointers at least. Are they actually part of your head? Or will they come off like a helmet?'

'I am weary of questions about my appearance,' replied Herne, 'and I do not remember your grandmother.'

'She was a funny old woman,' Meadmore snickered. 'She had long grey hair which she used to twist into a spike, then stick it fast with goose-grease, so that she looked like a unicorn. Did you know that she'd cure warts by eating dandelion heads? And she'd always leave out a quart of milk for the fairies.'

Herne gritted his teeth. 'Please do not burden me with more details about this woman and her disgusting, superstitious habits. Because I dwell in the woods, people judge me all wrong. They think I'm interested in roots and vegetables and goblins and elves. Nothing could be further from the truth. I dislike elves – their pointed ears oppress me. I do not like goblins either – they make uncouth sounds while eating. And I hate ghosts who have no function beyond glimmering. No, I am modern-minded and practical in outlook and would like to learn about metalwork and book-keeping. I also wish to travel. But above all, I wish to enter the world of men. Yes, I wish to shed these horns that make me look like a cuckold, and walk forth unfettered and free.'

'It is not possible Herne,' I told him. 'Your identity is written down like the rings of the oaks.'

'If I shed these horns,' said Herne, 'I will lose my power and gain my freedom.'

Again he brandished his club and let out a panting groan. The same stag came bounding out of the trees. This time Herne struck the ground twice, and the stag – as if the impact had been on its living flesh – let out an an even louder belling. Instantly four red and white oxen came tramping into the clearing, huge beasts with shaggy flanks and sharp brown horns. They were yoked together and wore silver collars. Steam arose from their flanks which were still glistening from the recent rain.

Herne stalked over to them, drawing up a length of rope that ran from their halters. He walked over to a massive oak, shouting to Meadmore, 'O vain and foolish knight, I wish you to dignify your life by doing one useful deed.'

Meadmore gave a terrier-nod of his head. 'I will do anything to assist you, sir. My grandmother said...'

'Bind me to this tree!' roared Herne. 'Use my chains – wrap them round the trunk and over the lower boughs.'

I tried to restrain him, but Meadmore obeyed, winding the chains around the stag-god, tying him fast to the oak. Herne called the oxen over. Taking up their harness, he lashed it around his horns. 'At last I shall free myself of these ridiculous protrusions,' he muttered. 'I will be able to live a normal life – buy a tavern in the city, sell cider, filberts and eels.'

Meadmore stood back. I tried to dissuade Herne from his rash course, but he snarled at me and I backed away.

'Away! Away!' he called, geeing up the oxen.

The four huge beasts plunged forward in unison tightening the harness. Groaning and steaming, they strained and pawed, their broad hooves sinking into the earth. Herne's head, guyed up to their muscled collars, was yanked forward, and the chains binding him sank into his flesh. Grafted deep into his skull-plates, his antlers resisted the effort to pull them free. Knots of muscles and veins stood out like cables running down below the ears to the mossy chest.

Herne let out another painful shout, urging the oxen to pull harder. Again the massive beasts jerked and laboured, and Herne's neck began to distend. A screaming of flesh and then a gulping shriek – the tendons exploded with an elastic lash of gore! The head tore free of the shoulders, spattering blood and gristle, and was borne along by the charging oxen who tramped towards the trees. The great horned ball clanged against trunks and roots, bounced along, scarring the ground like a ploughshare. Shadows closed over it and the oxen were lost in the shade of the oaks.

Silence drifted back. A light wind stirred among the foliage, making a noise like a dry, whispering laugh. A tit flew down from a tree and began pecking at a spot of red gristle. Shivering, I turned away, feeling like retching there and then.

I looked at Meadmore. His mouth still hung half-open and he drew a hand over his forehead, remarking, 'Faith Galahad, the fanaticism of these forest creatures! Why try to assume a role for which you are not fitted? I am a drunk and will always stay a drunk.' He peered at me under his pink lids; a glaze of yearning misted his eye. 'Have you got any wine with you? This fearful thing has brought on the thirst.'

Feeling nauseated and low of spirit, I walked over to Larkspur, unpacked the pitcher of wine and offered it to Meadmore. Trembling, he took it to his lips and sucked and swallowed like a baby at the breast. Although I despised him a little, the horror of what we both had seen had established a temporary rapport. We removed ourselves from the glade and found another site to set up camp. There we bedded down, kindled a fire, drank slowly until the sun set, night came and with it the moon, leaking a little silver amid all the gloom.

# 13

# EDMUND

Watching Herne's head being severed from his body did not prepare the way for a soothing sleep. Strange dreams visited me. The spires of Camelot rose up like bright fountains of stone. I saw fleetingly the face of Catherine peering from a corner of the battlements. But her welcoming, familiar features dissolved – instead there was the howling head of Herne, dripping gouts of blood, which sprang up and changed into flames! Fanned by a great wind, they began to spread and consume hut circles and farmsteads. Pigs, cattle and people fled before the all-devouring fire, and a harsh, knotted laughter seemed to follow in its wake. I saw my old master, Sir Porius Vrontigern, riding over a waste of burning fields, shaking his head sadly. Then I saw horned warriors riding amidst the same smoke and devastation; the tips of their spear-points glittered and their faces were like bronze masks. One came up to Porius and struck him off his horse and, on witnessing that indignity, I cried out, and then Sir Porius and the warriors were buried by a rolling wall of mist. The next moment I was falling back through my dream – fluttering and reeling like a leaf blown across a black gulph. I was being absorbed in a dark immensity, a fathomless void devoid of gods or certainties. The only meanings were fragile wisps of thought blown hither and thither…

'Galahad!' a voice called.

Trembling, I awoke and threw aside my riding-cloak. I raised myself from my dank woodland bed. There was little light, only gloomy ranks of treetops, with frayed patches of dull blue and grey where the sky leaked through. But I was unable to take in my surroundings because of the tight-coiled pain within my skull. Then I became aware of Meadmore's face anxiously hovering over mine. His eyes were sleep-drowsed, and his lower lip protruded sulkily.

'Is there no more wine, Galahad?' he asked. 'Did we drink the whole pitcher?'

'Go fetch some water, Meadmore,' I told him. 'The last thing we need is wine. We have surely performed our due devotions to Father Bacchus. What we need now is water in order to drink and cook.'

'I cannot drink water, Galahad. It makes my brain ache.'

'Your brain will ache, Meadmore,' I told him brusquely. 'If you do not obey me, I will bring down this large stone upon your bascinet.'

Giving me a bruised, disappointed look, Meadmore snatched up the water pitcher and walked away, arms swinging loosely. Like a small boy, he hated being reprimanded. I got up, my legs like dull wooden blocks, and went over and attended to Larkspur. First I fed her some grain and then removed particles of straw and grit lodged in her hooves. When I had finished, Meadmore was back and holding an empty pitcher.

'I told you to fill it, man.'

'I intended to, Galahad. But I have found this ruin, this immense castle, in the woods.'

I snatched the pitcher from him, saying, 'Meadmore, we cannot drink a building.'

He replied with ironic meekness. 'I am aware of that, Galahad, but large houses often have wells attached to them.'

Meadmore had a point. I went with him through the clearing to an earth rampart that was broken in places. A little further on there was a gatehouse, hunched and ruinous, like an embittered retainer. Through a rustling hide of ivy, you could make out arrow slits and a fragment of castellated parapet in which owls were nesting. From thence we passed under an arch and came to a long timber-and-stone hall with twin towers at the end. Traceried windows peered down – a pigeon surprised us, bursting out of a recess and scattering its agitation. Why, I wondered, had the place been abandoned? It breathed the folly of a single man's madness – an initiative that spawned no heirs or imitators.

'Have you been inside?' I asked Meadmore.

'I thought I'd wait for you, Galahad.'

The door had fallen from its hinges. Stepping over it, I entered a long, empty chamber that everywhere breathed the dank, sour smell of desolation. On the floor, cloths and animal skins lay strewn about, splashed with moist earth which had crumbled from the walls. Some weapons lay scattered on the floor: a round leather shield with a studded iron boss, a feathered lance, a short sword with garnets embedded in the handle.

'I do not like it here,' said Meadmore with a shiver. 'I have changed my mind, Galahad. I shall not help you look for the Grail. I want to look for something else. There's a certain cross that's missing at the Abbey of Linton. I think I'll go after that instead. It might not be such an important thing to look for as the Grail, but I'm not ambitious. If I find it, I'll feel I have achieved something in a small way. Then I'll settle down, find myself another woman, and grow vines. You know Galahad, I know the exact spot, Pilton, which has a stream running through a narrow valley, with steep slopes on the south side, ideal for cultivating grapes…'

'Meadmore, stop prattling! You will drive me mad!'

'Don't shout at me, Galahad. We all need to talk from time to time.'

His remark trailed off into an abrupt cry – his eyes stood out like studs. He backed away and worked his mouth soundlessly. I swung around and saw a young man in a doublet peering at us. Tall, slim and clad in stuffed silks, he had a pointed chin and auburn curls. His cheekbones were smooth-planed and delicate and his blue, incurious eyes held no warmth. He must have entered through a doorway to the left of the fireplace, for I could trace the marks of his feet in the dust.

Both Meadmore and I were struck dumb. We stared like gaping statues. The man looked back blankly. Silence gathered like a pool, only broken by the faint cawing of rooks in the elms beyond.

'Pardon me,' the young man began earnestly, 'before I introduce myself, I would like to ask you both a personal question.'

'Go ahead,' said I, taken aback.

Clearing his throat, he blurted out. 'Are either of you knights bastards?'

Such a strange manner of introduction took my breath away. 'Not to my knowledge,' I murmured.

'Faith, what does it matter!' said Meadmore with some of his old spirit. 'We all come out of the same door, whether's there's a nameplate on it or not.'

The young man gave a ferocious nod. 'Exactly. You have hit the nail on the head. Most perceptive of you!'

Meadmore frowned. 'What did I say then? I've already forgot.'

'You intimated,' the youth replied, 'that there is no inequality betwen those born in wedlock and those born out of wedlock, save for the backward laws of this land.'

'I agree most heartily,' said I.

'Good,' said the intense young fellow. 'At last I have found a sympathetic audience. You see, I maintain that it is not a slur on one's character to be born on the wrong side of the blanket.'

'Quite so,' said I, edging away from him.

'In my opinion,' he continued, 'the most auspicious conjunctions occur outside of marriage. Such couplings have an added zest – a spice and fervour – that is absent in the legitimate union of male and female. My father held the same view – by the way, did I tell you that I'm Edmund, unofficial son of the Duke of Gloucester. Look at me. I don't look bad, do I?'

'You are most handsome,' said I. 'But is your father still alive?'

He shook his head. 'Not to my knowledge.'

'What happened to him?'

He gave a brief, dry laugh. 'He fell down a well.'

'How so?'

'He was stalking a grouse and lost his way.'

'What was the well called?'

'The Well of the Broken Head.'

I nodded gravely. 'A most untimely descent.'

Edmund shook his head. 'Nay, 'twas his bath night.'

'Your attitude seems unfeeling,' said I.

'That is because I am an absolute bastard,' Edmund declared. 'Yet I shall always be grateful to my father. For when he begat me, at least his mind was engaged upon the job. I'm no fop conceived 'twixt sleep and wake.'

Meadmore nudged me and muttered. 'Galahad, shall we quit this place? I do not like this odd young fellow. He talks naught of wine and jousting, only of making two-backed beasts, and in a manner more befitting a tired tutor.'

Edmund moved his hands languorously over his body. 'Look at me. You can see that I am shapely: slim hips, crisp auburn hair, plump calves, a complexion as fresh as any girl's, and I have earlobes clean and pink as shells. Look, I can twitch them from side to side – a jester taught me that. These special abilities are granted to me because I'm a complete and absolute bastard.'

Meadmore yawned. 'All most diverting, I'm sure.'

'Many men of ferocity and distinction,' Edmund continued, 'fall into the category: Genghis Khan, Nero, Attila the Hun, Alexander the Great, Hrongar the Head-Eater – all were undoubted bastards. Also Socrates, Demosthenes, Ptolemy, Omtompetep the First, Julius Caesar, Heraclitus, Virgil and Wang Ho Topolong – he pioneered an early type of water-wheel!'

'I had no idea,' said I, 'You have certainly looked into the matter.'

Edmund smiled. 'I am compiling a 'Book of Bastards'.

'Can we not talk about something else?' grunted Meadmore. 'Is there not any drink in this place?'

'Come into the throne room, and I will see if there is any,' said Edmund.

We followed him inside. The throne-room was longer and broader than the main hall. The floor was paved with encaustic tiles and there was an oak table with bowls spread on it and a gilt bronze jug. At the distant end was a wall pierced by pointed arches upheld by blue marble columns. In the space between two pillars, I was able to make out a plasterwork relief of horses springing from waves.

I gestured at the carvings. 'What are these horses?'

'They tell the story of Lyonesse,' replied Edmund, 'the land west of Cornwall which was lost beneath the waves. One of the king's ancestors hailed from the drowned kingdom. He was resued by a swimming horse, and it was he who commissioned the work.'

'Of what king do you speak?'

'King Lear. This is his palace, although he has long renounced the throne.'

Edmund went up to an alcove which was screened by a dull red curtain. He pulled it aside, exposing a high wooden throne. It was painted blue, scarlet and gold, and carved with swags of fruit and foliage. At the base lay sprawled a blackened skeleton with its legs twisted and bony arms outflung. The skull wore a crown of gold leafwork studded with rubies.

I gasped. 'Whose body is that?'

Edmund replied casually. 'That is Sleedon, King Lear's son and successor.'

'How can he reign? He is dead – incapable of anything.'

'A most excellent qualification,' said Edmund with a thin smile.

'What happened to him.'

'Grievous tidings. You can read his history. I have set it down.'

Edmund walked away and came back holding a pitcher full of wine and some scrolls of parchment. He held out the wine to Meadmore who took it and then went across and gathered up three goblets which he filled. He brought them over with a composed smile, and the two of us sat down and quaffed, while Edmund read to us the following history with level complacency.

# 14

# LEAR AND HIS THREE SONS

T he dukes of Albany, Cornwall and Kent, together with their courtiers and serving-men, gathered at the palace of King Lear, who wished to make a most urgent proclamation. Rumour had it that, having reached an advanced age, he planned to retire and appoint a successor.

All the nobles waited with nervous expressions. Eventually Lear made an entrance. Clad in blue and gold swirling robes, all royally fleeced and lined, he stalked up to the throne. White-haired, intense, with furrowed forehead and aghast eye, he grasped the arms and lowered himself into place.

Beside the throne was a straight pole implanted in a box of earth, an object to which he seemed to attach importance, for before sitting, he caressed the top with his fingers, as though it were the symbol by which his royal authority and dominion were ratified.

'Long have I pondered metaphysics and philosophy,' he began. 'The problem of man's folly has long been uppermost in my thoughts. Why does he perpetrate strife and cruelty? Why does he seldom sun himself in the bowers of content? After lengthy meditation, I have concluded that the root of all evil is action. Action engenders foul deceits. Action engenders perjury and treason. Action is the canker which hath afflicted man since God plucked and moulded him from common clay. Man may achieve perfection only by doing naught. He who doeth naught breeds no ill-will – for all consequences are cancelled. The lazy man, therefore, is like unto this innocent pole, this scratching-post of the humble kine, that I keep at my side. Is not such stasis blessed, I ask? A still point 'gainst which the evil-doer may measure his wrong?'

Several courtiers nodded. Others let out murmurs of dissent, but Lear, ignoring such remonstrations, arose from the throne. He gestured to the figures of his three sons who gravely regarded him from their seats below.

'Age burdens me with feebleness,' he continued. 'As the body begins its slow hike deathward, I desire to cast off the cares of kingship and confer it on younger strengths. Therefore I will offer up my kingdom to one of my three sons assembled here, Bractactus, Congril and Sleedon, according to which hath done least to develop his talents. Bractacus, our eldest-born, you may speak first.'

Bractacus was a red-faced man with black hair and a suppurating left eye. Standing, he addressed his father with pride and confidence. 'Sire,' he said, 'I am as tardy a laggard as ever trod the earth. Above my bed is a hole through which the rain doth plenteously drip. Its pattering sorely vexes me and makes of my blankets a sorrowing sponge. Furthermore my Lord, this water doth plash and skip upon the ball of my eye – see how dim and cloudy it is! In time, this prattling, petulant leak will render me blind.  The water will gnaw deep into the marrow of my bones, and my body will become a senseless sack of chills and fevers.  Yet sire, rather than moving my head the littlest inch, or order a servant to block this naughty leak, I prefer to endure perpetual mist and ceaseless sneezing.  But soft, methinks I do digress too much, citing my worthless praise, and I must await the verdict of my loving father.'

Lear closed his eyes and nodded.  Then he arose from his throne and peered into Bractacus's grey and milky eye.  Satisfied, he walked back to his seat, muttering, 'Thou hast spoken well, Bractacus.  Thy laggardliness shines like a halo.  Well done, my son.  And now, Congril, what sayest thou?

'Sire,' said Congril, a plump man with a fluting voice.  'My brother, Bractacus, may indeed qualify as a laggard of distinction.  Yet compared with me he is a demon of industry.  Look at my hand here – 'tis a blunt and useless stump!  How came this so? I was sleeping in the woods upon a soft and mossy couch, listening to the trillings of a linnet, when this poor wight doth implant himself upon my patch.  In his hand he bore a mighty saw, all fretted and fanged like a shark's mouth.  This fearsome instrument he doth employ to chop down the tall oak's prime.  Sir, he saith, wilt thou move thy hand, else this cruel blade may sever and dismember its keen and pliant sinews? Nay, saith I, the day is bright, and the sun's ray do tenderly kiss mine eyelids, and I feel not disposed to move a fraction.  I would rather cast my hand to the birds that they may derive nourishment from its lily-pale and languid flesh.'

The King looked impressed at this.  He gave a nod and an approving grunt. Then he levered himself up, struggling with the obstinacy of his stiffening arms, and went forward and examined the severed limb.  After giving it several taps and probes, he was assured of its authenticity and slowly paced back to the throne, saying, 'Congril, thou art indeed a worthy sloth, and I commend thee highly for it. And now Sleedon, youngest of my sons, what sayest thou?'

Sleedon, a willowy and weak-voiced young man, made no effort at all to rise.  An infinite weariness was stamped upon his smooth and listless features.  As the King waited with some impatience, several times he opened his mouth, then closed it again, as if the effort of moving his lips taxed him to excess.

Finally he deigned to speak.  'Sire, I will be brief,' he said, 'for the slightest action of my jaws doth make my bones ache and my brain spin.  It may please my Lord to cast his eye upon my feet, which are swaddled and bandaged all over.  These are not the wounds of war, sire, but the delicious fruits of loaferdom.  I was warming my soles before the hearth, when a log fell away, burning my boots and making the feet therein sizzle and fry.  But rather than expend the effort of drawing in my legs, I let them linger among the nest of licking fiends, and now, my Lord, my feet are all burned away.'

Again the King crept forward to examine the damage.  Carefully he jabbed at the soiled, red-stained bandages that bound his youngest son's feet.  Then he ambled back to the throne, muttering, 'Thou speakest well, Sleedon.  Indeed thou art an honest waiter on Providence.'

Lear sat down and let his head fall forward, as if about to enter a deep slumber. Shutting his eyes tight, he gritted his teeth and snarled.  Then, clenching his fists, he beat the arms of his throne like a child having a tantrum.  His breath came harsh and hoarse, and, fixing his sons with a furious glance, he bellowed:

'O my three crafty and false-hearted sons! Thinkst thou that thy greybeard father is a dolt? Thinkst thou that I am like the loony bird that warbles vain and solemn nonsense to the moon? Thou hast employed thy glib and oily skills to deceive me! To puff thy profiles until they art naught but bags of wind. Ye would have me believe that ye are peerless princes of inaction, and yet, to reach this very palace, ye had to stiffen and flex thy legs, inhale the frisky wind, mount haughty steeds and ride forth upon the dusty road. Is that, I ask ye, typical of one who truly vegetates? Doth this solemn and silent post, that stands so faithfully at my side, jump upon a horse to make attendance at a state occasion?'

Bractacus and Congril remained silent at this accusation. Looking ashen-faced and furtive, they shuffled their feet and studied the floor. The courtiers mumbled among themselves, some conceding Lear his point, others wringing their hands in exasperation.

But Sleedon boldly answered his father.

'Sire, I did not urge into motion a single muscle to reach this hall. I was carried here by my servants on the silken divan that you see yonder. Furthermore, I am willing to offer myself up as a pawn to those very principles that I am accused of betraying.'

'Speak up, my son!' said Lear. 'Let me hear what plan you have devised.'

'I have told thee,' replied Sleedon, 'of my unflinching sloth that doth not balk at burning skin. With my kind Lord's permission, I propose to endure a most grim and frightful ordeal. I have brought here four stalwart servants to abet me. See, my Lord, how this very moment, they bear logs in their coarse, bearlike paws.'

The four servants came forward, arms laden with birch logs, which they set down on the floor before the King. Carefully they built them up cross-fashion, arranging them in a lofty pyre, and then placed on top a plain board, forming a kind of platform. Next one of the men strode away and came back with kindling twigs and a bale of hay which he tore apart and sprinkled around the base. Then all four of the servants went over to Sleedon, who had now repaired to the divan. With his eyes half-closed and his mouth slightly parted, he lay back like a languid caterpillar on a velvet leaf. The servants took hold of the corner-handles and raised the couch, faces solemn as pall-bearers, to the high platform.

Smiling faintly, Sleedon yawned and stretched out his legs. The four servants went away and came back carrying flaring naptha torches. Sleedon drooped a long, sticklike arm over the edge of the divan and flexed his small finger, signalling the servants to light the straw at the four corners of the pyre. Afterwards they stood around grim-faced and watched.

'Watch now, my Lord!' said Sleedon from the top of the burning pyre. 'If, after this ordeal, my sloth doth not move heaven by its proud, unyielding will, then let the sky go red as blood and a green sun arise on the morrow!'

First there came few sportive cracklings and then the flames fattened and leaped higher. Sleedon's entire form was almost lost behind a screen of pulsing orange and red. Flickering points of gold and white began to fasten and gnaw, first at the couch, and then at the bandages around his feet. When they caressed Sleedon's breeches and doublet, a frown did crease his brow, but he manfully fought against it and regained the mask of serenity and repose. His clothing was now patched with glinting flames; stray metal buttons, hitherto stitched to his garments, detached themselves and tinkled down among the lower logs. At this point, a deep groan did issue from Sleedon, who, slumped on the blazing couch, fought to arrest an involuntary flailing motion of his left arm. Eventually the rolling columns of smoke sent up by tbe blaze were permeated by this most foul broiling odour. Various courtiers raised linen kerchiefs and pressed them to their noses and lips. But they were unable to turn their heads from the spectacle, which transfixed them, as only gruesome things can. They coughed, spluttered, fanned the fumes with their arms, but refused to back away, their expressions an unholy brew of fascination and horror as they watched the flames dwindle and die. There was silence. Silence and a ripple of spreading shame. Then one man, the court victualler, stepped forward and let out an excited whisper and pointed. A patch of smoke drifted across revealing a loose-knit ebony skeleton sprawled among the charcoal and clinkers.

Clamping one palm over the top of his pole, Lear levered up his ancient frame once more. When he spoke his voice was loud, yet meaning seemed to linger feebly in its wake. 'O Sleedon,' he cried, 'I curse myself for ever doubting thee. Now thou art naught but juiceless bone, thy blood singed dry by ravening flames, let no evil befall thee, or malignant elf haunt thy witless peace. Thou hast proved thy worth indeed. Therefore, in the presence of God and this retinue of lords and nobles, I hereby appoint thee my heir.'

Leaving the throne yet again, Lear edged his way down to the charred carcase of his youngest son. Kneeling, and with great tenderness, he removed his crown and placed it upon the eyeless, distended and flame-blackened head.

'A remarkable story,' I told Edmund, when he had finished. 'But you have not told us what happened to King Lear.'

'He is still alive.'

'He must be very old.'

'No older than certain giant tortoises,' said Edmund. 'I'm told they reach a great age.'

'What is a tortoise?' asked Meadmore frowning.

'Tis a creature that creeps around with a shield on its back,' I told him.

Meadmore frowned. 'Faith, why does he do that?'

'He has no choice,' said I. 'It is fixed to him.'

'Galahad, do not mock me. I know well no such creature exists.'

'Meadmore, you drank at an inn called *The Elephant and Tortoise.*'

'By heavens Galahad, you are right. I remember now. Is not the name applied to a family of reptiles which have a bony box enclosing their bodies, short legs, horny jaws for cutting, and head, limbs and tail which can be drawn in and hid?'

'How did you learn all that about tortoises, Meadmore?'

'I was told about them by a mariner who had been to Greece and India and Africa.'

'What was his name?'

'Henry Shellover Parsons.'

Edmund coughed. 'Do you wish to meet King Lear?'

'Where is he living?' said I.

'In this palace. Come, I will introduce you. A delightful old gentleman.'

Gesturing us to follow, Edmund left the throne room and bounded up a stairway. At the top was a hatch which he opened and entered by hauling himself up by the elbows. Climbing up behind, Meadmore and I found ourselves in a huge and gloomy loft with braced arches. Attached to a beam, a large cage hung from a thick goose-greased rope. The frame was square and of solid oak with black bars as thick as my wrist. Inside was an old man who looked so frail that one could barely believe he was alive. He was dressed in nothing save for a soiled grey loin-cloth, and around his neck dangled an impressive gold-chased medallion which made his wasted frame seem even skinnier. Gaoled eyes stared out from the pouches of pale skin. There was a basin of water beside him and a hunk of bread which was pecked at the corners. In his hunched immobile pallor, he reminded me of a plucked, life-less chicken, and his gaze was turned in on a world that was inaccessible.

'See!' pointed Edmund. 'There is the King. I keep him in this cage.'

'Is not that cruel?' snarled Meadmore.

'No, he is content up there,' replied Edmund. 'So long as the cage is cleaned and the water replenished.'

'Yes,' I argued, 'but what sort of life is it for the poor fellow?'

Edmund shrugged. 'He gets much pleasure out of music.'

'Music!' I exclaimed.

'Yes, music!' repeated Edmund. 'I will put on a show for you.'

Excited at the notion, he took down from a ledge a large square box that he placed on a trestle-table. He took off the lid, showing us a block of polished wood, to which a wooden, revolving wheel had been attached. Instead of paddles the wheel was hung with many little squares of stained glass, coloured orange, blue, red, yellow and emerald green. Behind it was a mounted cube of glass that hoarded the sunlight coming from a porthole in a wall behind, and in front was mounted a big lens that was stuck on to the tip of a hollow pole.

Next Edmund stretched up his hand and unhooked a drum hanging from the side of the cage. He slapped it a few times, crouched down, placed it on his knees, then began playing, maintaining a swift, insistent beat. High up in his cage, Lear's misty eyes flickered and his tongue hung out like a leaf. Stiffly he arose and began to stretch his arms and sway his hips very slightly. What followed was not truly a dance, more a dazed, feeble groping around a tiny compass. It was like watching a man struggling against the final stages of paralysis.

Then Edmund walked across to the wheel with painted glass on it and set it spin-ning. What magic we then witnessed! As each revolving piece of glass rattled into position, a swarm of quick-changing lights lit up the cage. It was as if a succession of beating, quivering, many-hued shadows were passing through. Edmund went back to his drumming, quickening the rhythm. Whereupon the King was seized with true agility. It was as if the fleeting dyes and splashes of colour restored his health. He jerked his legs, clawed and weaved as glinting aureoles of red, yellow and green trapped him in motion. The shifting hues dappled his ancient frame. Every so often he would look at the changing patterns on his skin in a delighted way. The cage began to sway and the King had to steady himself by grasping the bars. The percussion got louder, thunderous, hailstone beats merging into one prolonged crescendo. This excited the King who managed to sway his hips, stick out his abdomen and flutter his hands about in a teasy way. But despite these digital enticements, he fell a long way short of a dancing girl proper, and I cannot say I liked what he had put on for us. To end the business, Emund steadied a single hot white light on him whereupon he stepped forward, froze stock-still, blew us a few kisses, and then, with painful rigidity, raised one bony knee and attempted a hop. The effort proved excessive – he tripped and banged his head against the bars. With a muffled cry, he slumped to the floor, a tiny smear of blood on his forehead. Edmund responded with a climactic crash of his palms on the drumskin.

For a while Lear lay still, a huddle of wasted limbs. Then he raised his head – his face was like a broken fruit bereft of human expression. Casting the drum aside, Edmund walked over to the corner of the gable and removed an apple from a barrel. He took out a knife, peeled it, sliced it into segments and then went over to the cage.'

Edmund smiled. 'You've danced well today, King. Here is your reward.'

He reached up and pushed a bit of apple into Lear's hand. The King took it, clenched it possessively, as if it were a living creature that might fly away. After a while, he opened his palm and gave it a long and curious stare. But soon he lost interest in the apple, dropped it and began to pluck at a few white hairs growing under his armpit.

# 15

# THE WICKER MAN

E dmund, finishing eating, leaned back and shifted his legs restlessly. Catching his distorted reflection in a pewter salver, he gazed like Narcissus, lost in a delicate swoon of admiration, and then, conscious of his role as host, poured out more wine from the jug. 'Why do you want to obtain the Grail?' he asked.

'Arthur requires it,' I told him. 'He thinks it holds some vital principle that eludes us.'

Meadmore yawned and pushed his plate away. 'I am tired, Galahad, and I for one do not want to see the Grail. The very sight of the vessel is said to blind you – blind you! Faith, what's the use of that? Unless you wish to blunder around like a bat for the rest of your life, pleading for alms and saying, 'I am very holy – I've seen the Grail!' And d'you know how men will act? They will cry – *Away cringing loon! T'was not the Grail that struck you blind but the Lord himself who saw you spying on some nuns bathing in a stream.*'

'You are cynical about everything, Meadmore, because you only feel strongly about wine.'

'You do not want the Grail, Galahad. I have heard you say as much.'

'It gives shape and purpose to my gallopings.'

'The Grail is God's bone,' sneered Meadmore. 'And you are the proud pup who chases it.'

Edmund cleared his throat. 'I have heard that Prastigatus, the high priest of the Brigantes, has viewed the Grail at least once.'

'And how,' asked I, 'does he know this is our Grail?'

Part of the problem with the Grail was singling it out the unique vessel from the variety of basins, cups and receptacles various tribes held 'holy' or precious in their diverse regions. If I'd managed to retrieve all of them, I'd have returned to Arthur rattling and clanking like an overburdened tinker, and that is why I doubted any findings or reports that circulated amid the pagan tribes.

Edmund seemed amused. 'Ask him yourself. He claims that, in certain rites, all beliefs mingle and a Druid can see things a Christian venerates and the other way round.'

'I hope this is no idle rumour.'

Meadmore shook his head. 'If hopes were horses, beggars would ride.'

'Silence Meadmore!' said I, irritated by his perpetual sneering. 'You've a little black dog on your shoulder today.'

'Prastigatus spoke of a sacred cauldron,' said Edmund, 'which certain wise men claim to be the Grail.'

I gazed hard at Edmund whose expression was blank to the point of boredom. 'Where do I find this priest?'

'In the wild lands to the north,' Edmund replied. 'Follow the river valley down to the lake and then enter the hill country north of Gordalis.'

Meadmore shook his head. 'I despair of you, Galahad. Do you know what my advice is? Stop chasing the Grail and wait – yes, wait – and let Grail come to you. If you are worthy of it, it will appear, and if it doesn't you've lost nothing and gained a little peace.'

The next day Meadmore and I, thanking Edmund for his hospitality, left Lear's ruined palace. Setting out at dawn, we reached the edge of the forest by the after-noon. Beyond lay the hills and moors of the far north, sliced by wild gorges and roaring torrents, where cattle thieves hid their booty and the soil was thin and acid.

Meadmore shivered. 'What a land! No fat sheep, no tilled fields, only the wind screeching like a banshee.'

'You've never travelled in the northlands before, Meadmore. You've confined yourself to the warm southern lands.'

'Not true, Galahad, not true.' Meadmore shook his head vigorously. 'Five years ago, I travelled through the mountain country of the Votadini, riding for many days until I came to this forest. In the middle of all the trees was a spring which lay beside a cave. When I entered, this most ferocious red dragon came at me and blew out a rasping sheet of flame. But I parried it with my shield and smote off its head with my sword. Then I came to another chamber, guarded by another red dragon, of lesser stature than the first, which straightway engaged me in combat. I smote off its head too. Then I walked on and reached a third chamber, where there was a yet smaller dragon, and I did the same. And so I went on, finding chamber after chamber, smaller dragon after smaller dragon, smiting off each head in turn, until I came to this grotto where there was naught but a tiny lizard.'

'What did you do then?' asked I.

Meadmore gestured emptily with his palm. 'I fed it a few crumbs and left it as it was. You see, I had come to the conclusion that there were more important things in life than decapitation.'

His words were drawn short by a hammering blast. He raised an elbow to guard his face, and his horse moved over slightly. The wind assailed us like a bodiless legion whose power was perpetually replenished by invisible reserves of pure force. My eyes began to water in the unrelenting blast. For we had now climbed to the highest point of the moor, marked by a small blue pool, fed by a spring. There was a white post standing nearby into which coins and bits of rag had been nailed. People left such pitiful trinkets, hoping destiny might shed a tear or two in their direction, cure their palsied limbs or provide them with little bounties of cheese and milk. 'No beast,' I thought, 'would ever demean itself that way.'

We gazed northwards and saw rolling away, like row after row of massive green dunes, the gloomy peaks of the Cheviots, plumed with mist, sprinkled with snow. Proud, dreaming hills, their shadowy streams and enclaves seemed not to bear the mark of man. I knew the Romans and Pictish tribes had passed through, but I could not imagine wandering happily in them. There would be no fingerposts pointing the way to settlements and inns, no friendly tinkers trudging their paths or kindly shepherds offering hospitality. There would be naught but heavy silence and the creak and plaint of the birds who favour such lonely spaces.

Meadmore halted his steed and lifted back his head. 'Here I part ways with you, Galahad,' he said, eyeing me defensively. 'This country is not to my liking. Besides, I am fearing for the health of my father, who may have caught a chill during these late rains. I will head back south. And if you find the Grail, you might mention in your dispatches that I helped you along the way.'

'Where is your courage, man?' said I.

'That is one thing that need not vex me,' replied Meadmore. 'When you are deemed truly worthless, men expect nothing of you. I am a man who has fallen far. There are no obligations and standards by which I need abide. Farewell Galahad, do not think ill of me. Where would the world be without cowards? We are the yellow backcloth against which the scarlet deeds of glory shine.'

He leaned over a little and his horse swung round. He raised one hand in a parting gesture and began to canter down the slope. The drumming hooves faded into echoing thuds. I watched Meadmore diminish into a glinting speck, climbing over the brow of a hill and out of sight. A chill slime formed on my skin. I had never felt so utterly abandoned. Tired as I was of Meadmore's indecisive ways, I felt shock at his sudden desertion. It meant that I would have to brave out the wild lands alone. Meadmore was weak, yet even weakness can be invigorating, if accompanied by a certain quality of character. Now I had nothing to abide by but my lonely resolve.

Following Edmund's directions, I found the place above Gordalis, a wattle and thatch village. I asked a tribesman where I might find Prastigatus. He pointed to a high hill above the byres and huts where the Brigantes were erecting a Wicker Man, a device in which they sacrificed slaves and prisoners in order to placate their gods. I took Larkspur up the steep slope and there, on a small flat-topped spur, saw an immense figure, a massive fretwork of boughs and branches, all interwoven to form the shape of a man, anchored at the base with ropes and stakes.

On a hillock, fifty paces away, stood the priest, Prastigatus, clad in a white robe that was flapping so much he had to restrain it with his hand. Small and knotty, arms and face stained red with cockle-dye, I could not separate his features. His chin rested on a snake-headed wand over which his hands were clamped. His expression was numb as a mask, the face of a man grown dogmatic by ritual, frozen stiff by years of rote and custom.

About fifty tattooed warriors were prodding the prisoners with spear points, forcing them to enter. Ladders were propped against the latticework; platforms were arranged inside to accommodate the maximum number. Soon it was crammed with felons who were protesting and squabbling among themselves. A few armed men with torches of burning pitch strolled around the feet which were banked up with twigs, straw and kindling. Tiny fires, starting at the base of the body, were growing in height and breadth and starting to engulf the frame.

I braced myself for the horror about to unfold.

An exultant shriek split the air and left it trembling. I stiffened with fear – for it did not hail from any of the victims but came from behind. Looking over my shoulder, I saw a startling sight that took my mind off the flaming horror I was witnessing. It rolled back the screen of the years and uncovered a past I thought unreachable, a place or haven I'd believed then was permanent, but had long deferred to change and transformation. It brought back that ancient grey-windowed manor with its red-tiled roof, walled garden and deep clear well, at Dykesyat where I was born, and the memory of my father – always fussing and stern and yet never denying what I truly wanted – piling up the bricks in the yard to make a dovecote.

What I beheld was an upturned female form, her woollen-clad legs turning over like spokes in a wheel, her frayed and mud-splashed skirts falling away from her pale but unclean thighs.

It was Amelia, our former serving-girl, greyer and older than I remembered her, but still cartwheeling with vigour and whooping and cackling with delight. Behind her, looking even greyer, yet lean as a root from unceasing exercise, was the armless man, his knees still cranking along determinedly and his vegetable face still moist with desire. All those years, I thought, all that chasing, yet he had never managed to catch her. He had kept the wick of his lust aflame by anticipation alone. They ran past Prastigatus and myself, quite unconcerned by our perplexed glances. It was as if the worlds of escape and pursuit were separate realms of delight and never in need of meeting.

Prastigatus craned his neck and stared. He had suffered a jolt, an affront, yet an honest depiction of the way of things are – that, side by side with travail and suffering, the village swain pursues his nearly obtainable lass. I had an impression it stirred him personally, as he watched the armless man scurry up a narrow valley and over a heathery hill, growing smaller, until he resembled a moving pole, and Amelia a mere sketch of a starfish slowly turning. I tried but did not divine meaning from the spectacle.

Meanwhile the flames enfolding the Wicker Man grew and stretched upwards, like swaying draperies, quivering spires. Heat quickened; the prisoners bawled their agony to the sky. As screams broke around Prastigatus, like the cries of mad, burning birds, his expression became alert, almost excited, believing from the mouths of dying men came messages from the gods.

A cloud moved over, dense and dark like the cloak of Odin. The sun's rays choked and struggled. Long, drowning shadows buried the hills and valley. A silence like that of a warrior half-drawing his sword – a gritty hiss of steel, the violence lingering in the halted gesture. At my back, I heard a bird – a thrush perhaps. It was caught up in some tiny, hard, ecstasy of itself, a piercing, prattling song that foolishly zagged about. The silly little air went on and on as the fire and smoke spread and the odour of mortality tainted the atmosphere.

Leaving Larkspur, I went over to Prastigatus, who was scratching an enflamed patch above his ear with his snake-wand. But then, on getting close, I let roll a powerful oath – Sodding Oddbods! I *knew* him only too well, but by another name, that short, clenched figure with suspicious eyes and scabbard-slit of a mouth.

'Dylfric!'

'Galahad!'

He was much the same, agelessly aged, only his stare was shiftier and his stance more hunched.

'What mean you by this ghastly spectacle?'

He took offence at my words – guiltily, I thought.

'*Ghastly*? I have seen the light, Galahad.'

'*Light!*'

'I was converted.'

'How?'

In a covert, halting tone, as if each word cost a lot of conscience, Dylfric replied. 'You recall when I last parted from you, Galahad? On the road to Ducklehurst, riding with Black Susan on my lap? I had only gone five miles when there was a peal of thunder and I was thrown from my horse. I was lying on my back, and the next moment the grass around me was burning with a flame that was white and pure, yet absolutely cold. And then a red-robed angel reared out the conflagration, saying aloud – Dylfric! Go forth and spread the flame! Light the fire of truth! Burn your message in men's hearts and minds. Let the fire of your spirit kindle hope!'

'Is that all?'

'Yes, ever since burning's been my passion.'

I thought that an inflammatory remark and told him so whereupon he began to defend himself.

'Galahad,' he said, pointing to the prisoners, 'those felons are being liberated. As the flames enfold them, Paradise opens its door!'

'If you truly believe that, Dylfric, ignite yourself, so that you might share their pleasure.'

'The pain is of their devising,' he insisted, 'because they fight their fate rather than embrace it. Think of water in a pot, with heat underneath it, how joyfully it bubbles!'

But I, having none of this, berated him.

'I am disappointed in you, Dylfric, starting out a Christian and ending up a fire-worshipper! Father would be appalled! Why, compared with you, that armless man is a saint, pursuing a simple, honest lust, that's all, while you, well, you've become a monster!'

This stung Dylfric who turned on me.

'What nonsense you prattle, Galahad! Us Druids do not put on shows just for ourselves. Look around! See what bright raiment the people are wearing – how the children are smiling! This is no gross gathering, but a popular *do* wherein traders meet other traders, sell trinkets and souvenirs, women show off their beads and fashions, and the lonely find new friends and, at the same time, should they so wish, enjoy the fiery spectacle put on for them. You see, for ordinary folk, Galahad, few things are more heartwarming than deciding on a common enemy and setting him a-crackle! Such customs bring people closer, and it's only the likes of you, and those kill-joys at Arthur's court, who'd wish to suppress it, not because it would make for a happier world, mark you, but because you hate the thought of country folk enjoying simple pleasures!'

I was taken aback – for what Dylfric said was partly true. No, I *had not* taken in the surrounding constituency, only perceived it in accordance with a judgment already lodged in my head. But now I looked and saw spread over the hillside, in knots and huddles, many groups ranged around tables, cages and shelters. I saw women, young and old, in vegetable-dyed cloths of red and green, with beads and twinkling bits of metal in their hair, busily chatting, and then there were traders arranging pots and vessels, children, bright-eyed as young rabbits, running around and hiding between the stalls, and vendors proclaiming the virtues of their dark, unsieved ales – a festival indeed!

The black cloud drifted away; the setting sun gaped through. Ebony-ribbed and ominous, the skeleton of the Wicker Man lay silhouetted against the sky, a malevolent deity in its death-throes. The air crackled and hummed – twisting orange tongues skimmed up the stagings to the crown. A fretted edge of flame glowed like bright braid along the shoulder spars and straw-stuffed head. As it crackled and spat, the wood twisted to form cindery mutations, and around it smoke and black ash whirled like a storm of ravens. Logs fell, platforms crashed down, charred things tumbled out, setting me thinking of Sleedon, son of Lear, who had voluntarily selected such a fate.

A drubbing of hooves – steady as a drumbeat. I gaped askance. It came from the valley beyond. The noise mounted and grew thunderous. What new monstrosity was signaled by this? Dylfric was alarmed – so was I!

Four huge steaming beasts came pounding over the brim of the hill. They seemed to be towing something like a big craggy ball with branches growing out of it. Moving fast and growing larger with each stride, I recognized the four red and white oxen dragging the head of Herne the Hunter. Drawing up beside the Wicker Man, they halted abruptly, so that the head, taken up with the slack, bounded and clanged about until it was restrained.

Herne's cranium was bruised and muddy from all the rushing and bashing, but otherwise did not appear seriously damaged.

Gazing at the burning effigy – with raging disapproval, I thought – he let out a roar loud enough to rend a mountain. Whereupon, in obeisance, the clouds bunched up, dark and dense, then cracked like a pane of black glass. Next it was as if cataracts had been unleashed, a drenching downpour – not rain, more gushing torrents! – that seemed to concentrate around the Wicker Man. The big, blazing thing hissed and steamed; the flames were smitten and doused by a battering, shattering wetness. Soon it was all put out, leaving the wretched effigy engulfed in a dreary pall of wet smoke, cruel and harsh to breathe.

Hardly had I taken in this stupendous, heaven-sent spectacle than, with a brazen exhortation, Herne shooed the oxen on. The brawny breasts lunged forward, dragging his tumbling, bouncing head – chuckling and muttering to itself, as though possessed by some demon jokester! – around a projecting spur and out of sight.

As for the wet, shivering prisoners, they did not try to move or break out, but gaped with open mouths and giddy eyes. Their heads poked though the gaps and panels in the structure like geese at feeding time. The reversal of fortune had overtaken their cognition –their minds were still drawing breath. But then a little thin girl slave-girl let out a whoop of joy and slipped through her bars and started to climb down. The next instant all were funneling out, a web of arms and legs slithering down the colossal frame, the soldiers not bothering to obstruct them, assuming the sign from the heavens was equivalent to a pardon from the gods. They scrambled down the charred, half-slumped wooden shambles of a giant and, on reaching the base, fled through the crowd and over the hills, many burned, but weirdly jubilant – almost prancing! – at their deliverance.

Dylfric and I, barely moving, watched this.

'They have gone,' I said to him, 'into the hills.'

A long silence. Slowly the remains of the crowd took up their things and dispersed. One moment they were present, the next gone, melted into the green shadows. A white moon came out and nicked the pallor of the sky. A wind got up and the huge spaces gathered and whispered to us.

'As they go, so do I,' declared Dylfric and started to walk away.

Perplexed, I followed him for a while, stumbling occasionally and calling out, but he did not pay heed. He mounted the steep flank of the hill and began to climb. When he attained the ridge, he continued at a flat, even pace, down into the valley beyond. He took great care that he walked in an absolutely straight line. If a large boulder got in his way, he climbed over it. If a bush appeared, he would force his way through. If a stream, he would wade to the far side. Though he refused to look back or acknowledge me, I continued to call his name and trail behind until he came to large brown bog fed by a trickle of peaty water. It presented a dismal, flat surface, with a solemn sheen and a few scrawny reeds sticking through.

Without hesitation, Dylfric entered it, walking into the middle, his body steadily sinking, the agitated sediment belching indelicately, until the water stole up to his neck. Then he sank no more, but stayed absolutely still, his hard thin lips not moving, eyes fierce and steady.

'What are you doing, Dylfric?' I called.

He did not answer right away but paused and replied carefully: 'I am keeping my head above water, Galahad, that is all.'

Having no choice but to leave Dylfric in the mode of meditation he desired, I went back to Larkspur and ate a little food. I had found nothing pertaining to the Grail, leaving me still searching, but no nearer. I thought of the wild tribesmen of these harsh, marshy hills, praying to wood carvings and stones with holes in them. And then, in all honesty, I asked myself: Is Arthur better than these heathens? After all, he extols a kind of idolatry in demanding the Holy Grail. Well, say, if I find it and take it back to Camelot, what will it do, this sacred bauble? Will it make us better men? Will it make us a jot happier? Why do men place faith in objects? Is it because they have turned the land into such a sorry state by their own efforts that they have lost all self-esteem? Hence, instead of coordinating their wills – of making a prolonged, practical effort at righting things – they connive in the deception that such work can be achieved by the operation of a talisman or symbol. The pretend the inanimate can improve the lot of the vital. But a Grail cannot right the world anymore than a Cross or Sacred Lance.

Leaving Gordalis, I rode on, passing huts and homesteads, feeling more weary and lonely as the evening closed in. The northern moors were unrelenting, unforgiving. The winds blundered across the bare slopes and summits, hissing and rippling the coarse grasses, and I felt the clout of stinging hail and blown spray from cataracts. I drew my cloak tighter around my neck and thought of the massive log-banked fire in the feasting-hall of Camelot. But I could not sweeten my mood by dwelling on pleasant things, for every five miles I passed a Celtic altar, where a human head had been nailed to a post between a pair of gallowed ravens.

If you want anything, I thought, there is always a price, and that price is blood. To fertilise the soil, to placate the earth goddess, to stop the sun from burning us dry. And what is blood? Norsemen call it 'the sword's water' and others the 'fount' of life. Whatever blood truly be, the best place for it is under the skin of the person to whom it belongs. Why then this mania to release it, so that streams dribble crimson and men droop and die?

I looked up at the sky. A solitary buzzard was circling, a purposive speck which made me recall King Bladud. He wished to escape from dirt and bloodshed by inhabiting a region of pure air and cleanliness. Because our natural habitat is earth not space, we hurl our dreams of purity – our notions of a collective cleansing – into those loose, wind-riddled regions. We elevate clouds far above disease and death. In them we read a grace and benignity that naturally shapes itself to circumstance. Ever a-wandering, scattering and dissolving, they do not have one nature, but retain the possibility of change. They are like filmy vaporous spirits – that is why Bladud chose them as his companion-element. Did he succeed in finding a palace of the gods in the skies? Did it embody higher principles? Or do identical hungers – for blood, power, authority – dominate the things of air? The buzzard lazily dropped to the earth, plunged upon some vole or shrew, and flew away with its tail limp in its beak.

# 16

# THE SINGING DOG AGAIN

The second day after Meadmore left was even more depressing, a day of fruitless interviews with swineherds, priests, madmen. No sign of the Grail, and I was interrupted several times by men who called themselves knights. A man called the Green Knight offered to fight me, then a Red Knight, then a Blue Knight, then a Yellow Knight, and then a Black Knight. Naturally I refused all five invitations. I was unable to understand the mentality of ruffians who acquire lurid suits of armour and hang around in meadows offering to battle with anyone who crosses their path. Can not more useful employment be found for such people? Can they not be set to work in the fields? Or better still, let them gather faggots for the elderly and infirm.

In the evening I set up camp and lit a fire beside a stream that raced quickly over smooth black slabs of rock. It was a bleak, boggy spot, and after a short while it began to rain. Darkness fell, the rain drifted away, and the stars appeared like little silver pinholes. I shivered, as the loneliness hugged me close. I thought about Catherine and the warm southern lands around Camelot. I could not get to sleep. No longer did I believe that I would find the Grail.

At the height of my misery I heard a familiar sound.

'Woof! Woof!'

Startled, I glanced up. Two thoughtful brown eyes were hovering above the fire. Gradually a shaggy black mist formed around it, and then four hairy legs dropped down and touched the earth. It was the giant dog of Wimble Toot.

'I thought you had gone to your canine heaven,' said I.

'The kennels of eternity are full of combed spaniels and ladies' favourite greyhounds, and I got tired of the noise they make. They yelp, Galahad, yelp. I like to hear a good deep bark, you know my meaning.'

I nodded, still feeling glum.

'I saw you down here,' the dog continued, 'and I thought Galahad could do with a bit of company, and so I decided to go a-ghosting again.'

'Before you entertain me, kind dog, will you tell me whether I'm on the right track? For the Grail I mean?'

'The Grail,' replied the dog, cocking its leg and spurting mist, 'lies at the end of your journey.'

'Thank the Lord for that,' said I.

'Do not think, Galahad, that I do not understand this quest of yours. My master once gave me this marvellous juicy bone, and somehow I lost it. Believe me, I searched for it high and low and still look for it even now – and me a ghost! Yes, I understand the religious impulse.'

I nodded. 'Is there a meaning to life, do you think, dog?'

'I do not know, Galahad. That is rather like asking the meaning of water to a fish. Life is the element through which we swim.'

'That is a most intelligent remark.'

'Here, in the spirit world, I can no longer chase bones and sticks uphill and down dale – it is not seemly – so I read philosophy.'

'And what have you learnt?'

'That the earth may be round.'

I laughed. 'What an extraordinary notion! If that was so, we'd be clinging to its sides like flies on a wall.'

'No, that is no so, Galahad, there are forces that stop that happening.'

'This conversation is getting too deep,' said I, 'and I do not want it to get around to God, for He, being everywhere, easily takes offence. Let us consider other matters. For instance: What are your happiest memories, dog?'

The big dog slapped his tongue around his nose ruminating. 'The best time in my life was when I was a young pup and used to play in the courtyard of my master. The sun always seemed to be shining, and sometimes I'd lap up a puddle by the pump or sniff around the stables. Other times I'd chase a cat, or jump after a flitting butterfly. My early days seemed to be bathed in the halo of romance, Galahad. I shall never forget the time when I was introduced to King Cedric's hunting-bitch. Believe me, I was most sorely tempted, but I did hold back – for the sake of my master's reputation. But it was far from easy. You see, you are only human, Galahad, and you cannot comprehend the depths of passion a dog feels when he meets his one true bitch.'

'You are a most poetic hound,' said I.

'Music, poetry and sniffing – these are the things I love,' the dog mused.

I smiled. 'You're a cheerful old dog.'

'I think,' responded the dog thoughtfully, 'that a sense of humour is a highly important quality, both in life and death.' Slowly he raised himself up on his hindlegs, asking, 'And now, what would you like me to sing, Galahad?'

'Anything, dog, with the exception of *My Dear Old Headhunting Mama*. I never want to hear that tune again.'

'Nor I,' agreed the dog. 'No Galahad, I will sing for you the fisherman's song, *Tamburlaine the Trout*.'

'I do not know it.'

'You never studied music properly,' said the black dog.

He lifted his big blunt head to the stars and released a series of deep melodious howls. I listened to the rich and tuneful notes, and my mind revived. Like a fish through a sunlit stream, it flitted over cascades, down through willow groves and cressy shallows, finally out to the limitless sea, where it was absorbed by shuddering surf, and there fell fast asleep.

# 17

# VIKINGS

S hortly before dawn, I was aroused by men's voices, low, boastful and threatening. The ghost-dog had vanished. Strange how, the very second I woke, I missed the friendly, shaggy creature! As a boy, I had owned a large black dog as a pet. Often, I would go to him, bury my face in his fur and hear from within his pounding heart, steady as the dragon-heat of the earth, and get comfort from it. But the dog died many years ago, and I buried him on the slopes of Glastonbury Tor.

So had the ghost-hound of Wimble Toot come back and spoken? Or was it only my loneliness reaching out and bringing back dreams and secret companions? Some philosophers say that everything lies there, in the kingdom of the mind, whatever one needs, dreams and desires. There are even heretics who say this whole world – all its races, animals, plants and appearances – are the dream of a Master-Demon and when he awakens all of it will vanish. But I can only venture so far, for I am a knight, not a thinker. I suppose the dog had departed somewhere. Where was he now? Kennelled in oblivion? Barking in the half-light of the shadow realm?

No matter, the sky was still dark – no embers of dawn broke the veil of brooding black. I sat up and cast off my blanket. The voices rose and moved among the leaves and boughs, with bursts of urgency relapsing into laughter and repose. Who would be talking at this hour in such wild lands? Robbers? Shepherds? Whoever they were, they were burning something – drifted smoke from their fire smote me awake. I eased myself out of my rough bed and moved over to a clump of elms.

From the shelter of the trees, I peered out on a campfire. Flickering, scarlet and orange spires threw patches of light on the faces of three Norse pirates who were grouped around it talking. Their manner of speech was confidential, but I could tell they were restraining a pulsating excitement. I sensed that the day had far exceeded their expectations. They had just finished a side of venison, which they had eaten off golden salvers, and lying to the side of them was a vast ecclesiastical treasure horde: a gilt shrine, a lofty cross of ivory and gold, croziers, candlesticks, embroidered silk tapestries and a oak screen carved with niches occupied by the twelve apostles. It would have taken ten ordinary men to carry such plunder away.

Listening to their words, I gathered that they were celebrating a successful raid on a coastal settlement. The largest of them – Skullsplitter they called him – was dressed in purple and gold bishop's robes with a mitre on his head. What cathedral had he sacked, I wondered? The others, highly amused by his fancy dress, reeled about pounding the earth and laughing.

Skullsplitter grunted and exclaimed, 'Odin's blood! That was a good throw – did you see it, Olaf? At thirty paces I hurled the axe at the priest. I got him plumb in the forehead. His skull cracked open like a casket and out jumped his brain like a grey frog!'

A loud guffaw at this, and then Olaf, plumper and darker than Skullsplitter, remarked. 'I had almost every living woman in that village – from kitchen scullions right down to the thegn's wife! I threw her across the table, and made the thegn wait on me with food and drink as I paid my respects.'

The third Norseman, Eric, was thin and fine-featured. He laughed dutifully but then his eyes grew solemn. 'That is all very fine, Olaf,' he replied. 'Like you, I enjoy my share of burning, raping and pillaging, but I do think that Odin, in his eternal wisdom, meant us to develop other faculties. A higher type of wisdom exists which goes beyond the earthly pleasures of guzzling and lusting.'

Olaf frowned. 'Soon be time to pitch the cables and quit these shores,' he remarked, as if he did not want to be drawn into more thoughtful discussion.

A light wind stirred the leaves above me. I shivered and clenched myself. There was a loud barking and a swishing of foliage. A brown wolfhound streaked through the beeches, flashing a constellation of fangs. The breeze had carried my scent. I drew back but it gripped my leg and began wrenching. Cursing, I tried to kick it away – but it was too late. Already the Norsemen were bounding to their feet. Breaking into the glade, they encircled me with malign, scornful expressions. I reached for my sword, but the dog made a spring for my wrist, Skullsplitter grabbed me from behind, and there I was – a bundle of impotent fury. Hooping my neck in his hairy embrace, he tried to squeeze all the juice out of my throat. The other two aided him, taking each of my arms, and I was dragged towards the camp fire.

Olaf grinned. 'We have a living target for axe practice.'

'Unhand me, you oafs!' I snarled. 'I am from Arthur's court. If you as much as harm a button on my tunic, my fellow knights will avenge the indignity.'

Skullsplitter grunted and scratched his nose. 'Arthur's court, eh? What are the pickings like there? This Arthur, does he have much gold? What of his serving wenches – are they comely?'

I ignored this and stared back defiant.

'A quiet chap, isn't he?' said Olaf. 'Raven got your tongue, has it?'

'I do not exchange words,' I retorted, 'with human pigs whose troughs are filled with buckets of blood!'

A hissing intake of breath from Olaf. His eyes narrowed and his lip crinkled in a snarl. 'Axe practice for you, my friend!'

The three of them took me over to a tree. Skullsplitter produced a length of cord and winked, as though he had some trick in mind. While the other two held me firm, he wound it under my arms, around my waist, fastening separately my wrists, ankles and neck. So fierce and unrelenting were these bonds that I tried to spread out my muscles and gasp for air. My limbs were pulled out starwise and I was lashed to the tree like a human X.

Seething with anguish and humiliation, I stared down, spurning their attentions. But the three Vikings, heartless hulks that they were, were unaffected. They had the seasoned, animated looks of men about to engage in a habitual but moderately demanding activity. Olaf picked up a deerskin bag and removed three iron axes with painted bone handles and handed them to the others.

'I have sharpened them,' he announced, 'and now we will see how good we are at aiming in the dark.' He carefully paced out some twenty lengths from the tree and the others followed. Turning, they gave me glances of stern appraisal, holding up their thumbs and measuring my head relative to their shoulder heights.

Skullsplitter was the first to throw. Shutting one eye, he raised the handle, moved it from side to side, aligning the blade with my forehead. I gritted my teeth and closed my eyes.

'God, help me,' I thought.

The clenched hand scythed the air, the axe spun, flashing its colours like a kingfisher. A swish – a thud – an indrawn silence. Trembling, I opened my eyes and gasped. The axe was lodged beside my left ear. It had nicked the lobe, drawing a little blood.

And now it was Olaf's turn. He made less play with aiming, merely lifting the axe and throwing it with casual force. The blade whistled and struck home. When I dared look, I saw that it had embedded itself above my right ear, drawing still more blood that trickled down and stained my surcoat. I felt like whimpering with fear – why had I spoken such wanton words? Dealing with women, who will never cause me physical harm, I let words slip like honeyed droplets, and yet, when confronted with such murderous brutes, I cast around insults like seed.

'Your turn now, Eric,' said Olaf. 'We have pinned his ears. Now you must go for the bull's eye – see if you can make his brain do a frog-hop!'

Eric got up, looking uneasy and tired. I sensed a reluctance in the halting way he held himself and avoided staring directly at my face, a crude refinement which axe-throwing could not satisfy – my mind desperately struggled to find a ploy. As he aligned the axe-blade, I stared into his cold yet troubled eyes. He looked back at me and frowned. 'Keep your head straight.' He added more gently. 'Cheer up, knight, you're not being spreadeagled.'

'Hold your fire,' I called.

'Why should I do that?' he asked.

'I wish to tell you a story.'

'He wishes to tell us a story,' Olaf mocked. 'Friends, how privileged we are! For this we left home, crossed raging seas and fought like fiends. So that ninny of a knight should prattle on about damsels and dragons and men who say, *Gadzooks!* – *some evil villain has thrust a ferret up my corselet!*'

Despite the taunts, Eric paused, keeping the axe level with my head. It was as if his companions' urgings irritated him – forced him to weigh and quantify what he was doing. The silence swelled and gathered strengh. I dug my nails into my palms and whispered a prayer to every deity I knew. Skullsplitter grunted. 'Throw Eric – get it over with and then we can enjoy a song around the fire.' Olaf joined in, urging him to finish the business, but Eric did not budge. Slowly, with calm decisiveness, he lowered the axe to waist-level. 'Let us hear your story, knight, and make it good.'

At first I could find no words, only sounds scurrying at the back of my throat like frightened mice. Breathing deeply, I racked my head for a plot, a plan, a simple fable. But nothing came. My brain was a threadless tapestry, a vacant plot, a fruitless orchard. Eric raised his axe again, and then, quite miraculously, at the back of my mind, a bolt slid, a hinge moved. I heard my voice, as if it belonged to another, bubble forth like a spring.

'In Corinth four hundred years ago,' I began uncertainly, 'there was a most famous courtesan called Lais. Hearing that she was not only beautiful but skilled in conversation, the philosopher Demosthenes decided to hire her services. Demosthenes visited her quarters and knocked on the door. She received him with grace and gaiety whereupon he asked what was her charge. 'Ten thousand drachmas down,' she answered. And then Demosthenes turned away, remarking as he left her, 'Nay, I'll not buy regret at so high a price.'

I gulped the last words. There was a profound and hostile silence. Olaf looked at me with a kind of fierce incredulity. His face showed not a wrinkle of amusement. The scrap of classical wit meant nothing. Looking equally impassive, Skullsplitter frowned and scratched his chin.

'What's a courtesan?' he enquired.

'Any woman,' answered Olaf.

'No, it is not,' said Eric. 'They are women skilled in the arts of love who receive payment for their services.'

'Why did this Demos chap not rape her in the first place?' Skullsplitter asked.

'You cannot use force all the time,' said Eric.

'I do,' grunted Olaf. 'Any other way requires the patience of a stone.'

'An interesting tale all the same,' said Eric.

'It is a story worthy of a cream-faced loon!' snarled Olaf. 'Why, just for telling it, he deserves to be hacked into small bits and fed to the dogs.'

'No,' said Eric. 'It is a story with depth and human interest, and it has a quality of world-weary poignance.'

Olaf looked at Eric with wonderment. A frown snaked across his forehead and blended into an expression of genuine concern. 'Eric, my son, what has come over you? Using such words. You have been too much in the company of beardless minstrels who wince at the sight of blood and sing sagas in girls' voices.'

'He is the only one of you with any intelligence,' I told them. 'Listen to him, and set me free. I am as much a man as any of you. And I can prove it. Would any of you care to challenge me to a swordfight?'

Skullsplitter jumped at the invitation. Throwing off his bishop's robes, which collapsed around him like a gorgeous tent, he began to pull on his fighting uniform: steel cap, leather tunic and ring-mail. The other two went over to the tree and undid the cords that bound me. As I flexed my wrists and legs, sending the blood tingling through my numbed arteries, they cleared a space beside the fire.

'When I cut your head off,' joked Skullsplitter, 'I will use your skull as part of the figurehead for the longship.'

'At least, I'll get to see the world,' said I.

I was re-armed with a short Viking sword, for it was decided that the blades needed to be of equal length. We stepped into the space cleared for combat. No sooner was the sword in Skullsplitter's hand than his face set in a grim mould. Letting out a fearsome bellow, he began to bear down on me, angry as a wild boar with tail alight and toothache too. Immediately I felt relaxed. An old-fashioned beserker-style fighter, I thought, fair game for an energy-conserver like myself.

Doing a neat side-step, I slapped him hard on the back as he lunged past. He lurched and pulled himself up short. Turning, he repeated his bull-charge-and-yelling ploy. But I did a pretty dance around his fury, back-weaving, circling and parrying. Then he took so hard a swing at my head that he keeled over and fell. Taking his arm, I helped him up and asked whether he might not care to take a breather. He shook his head glumly. And so I stood back, waiting for him to pitch at me again. He drove down towards me, panting heavily, and I jumped aside and smote his helmet hard. There was a loud clang. His eyes dimmed to milky-blue, whereupon I delivered another hard blow and he fell at my feet.'

'Nice footwork,' said Eric. 'Poor Skullsplitter.'

'He wasted too much energy,' said I. 'All that shouting and charging exhausts one.'

'I will challenge you now!' said Olaf rising.

'No,' corrected Eric, who seemed to have an inexplicable authority. 'Let's have no more fighting. That's all we do. Let's have a gallon of good communion wine between us, and we can all enjoy some intelligent conversation with the knight. Let him know that Vikings can be hospitable and do not charge like the courtesan in the story.'

A friendly atmosphere then took hold. Each of us found a place around the fire. The communion wine was poured into goblets, the stolen chalices filled to the brim, and the four of us started to drink and converse. I told them about Arthur, son of Uther Pendragon, who had conceived a mad passion for Igerna, wife of Gorlois, the Duke of Cornwall. Using the wizardry of Merlin, Uther had disguised himself as the Duke in order to make love to Igerna at Tintagel, as a result of which Arthur was born. After they'd taken in that, I undercut Merlin's reputation, saying how foxed he'd been by the riddle I had posed, and then the Vikings in turn regaled me with stories of their land of pine forests and fjords, where perpetual snow lay on the mountains and there was plentiful fishing but little arable land. They described the bears and wolves that hid up in the mountains and the sun that shone at midnight.

'It is a wonderful land,' Olaf affirmed. 'Tall mountains reach up to the sky and are patrolled by ice giants who are almost as big. They use sharpened tops of fir trees to pick gristle from their teeth and small lakes to fill their drinking horns.'

I thought of Albion's wee fairies and elves who did little save sip bee nectar and winsomely flit from flower to flower.

Olaf made his eyes go big and spread out his arms.

'Huge fire-breathing dragons are found in our forests. When they pant, the sky becomes ablaze!'

Next Skullsplitter put in his groat of boasting, telling of the gods they worshipped, Thor, Odin, Baldur, Loki and Freyr, and showing little wooden images of each.

'Now,' he urged, 'tell me the names of your gods?'

'Gobwort, Festrule, Hubberdung, Tiptott and Krashingslash,' said I (fearing they'd think me a poor thing if I owned to only having one).

'Are they strong?' asked Olaf.

'Strong!' I echoed, as though the paltriest understatement. 'If the smallest of them whistled, it would split the world asunder.' Alas, I'd ventured too far – they turned doubting eyes on me. 'Fortunately,' I added, 'none are of a merry disposition.'

A silence and Eric enquired. 'You are seeking something?'

I told them of the Grail and its mysteries, how it only appeared under certain conditions, and often to those granted second sight.

Eric eyed me gravely. 'Do you know what the Viking does when he wishes to see Odin?'

I replied that I did not. Eric smiled, craned his neck and whispered to the others, adding, 'The time of year is right. We should be able to pick them by the dung heap over yonder.'

Their words perplexed me. I asked them to explain but they merely rose and walked away. 'We will be back soon,' said Eric.

They moved beyond the clump of beeches to a field. After a while, I was able to hear their voices exclaiming, 'Here are some large ones! Look I've found a whole colony! They should be truly potent about now!'

When they came back, they showed me their helmets. They were filled to the brim with tiny conical mushroom with purple-tipped caps.

'Pour the wine in the bowl,' Eric directed. 'Heat it up, then add the mushrooms to the brew, and we will see Odin and the knight shall see the Grail.'

'That seems an excellent arrangement,' said I.

The wine was heated and the mushrooms dissolved, and soon we were all dipping our chalices in and drinking it down. At first there was little noticeable effect, only my nose began to run and the cold night air ceased to chill my skin. Gradually this sensation of distance overcame me. I was less aware of being a body but more aware of being a mind. The faces of my Norse comrades became shiny and porous and their voices seemed like murmuring waves, breaking on the shores of my senses. It was as if I was floating upon a high cloud, and they were disembodied heads and sounds, coming at me from no rooted location, but from all around. Voices of air, tongues of space, eyes of light. But the torrent of words still poured out, hearty, animated and eager. Yet it was not like normal discourse – it did not proceed along natural lines. Topics would be broached, and then by dint of a shade, a nuance, a mood, they would be linked to something quite different. I remember telling Olaf about my horse Larkspur, and then I abruptly changed the subject, finding myself talking about Juliet Bors, but using such language as if she were the same as the horse.

And then I was laughing aloud, very heartily, but at nothing in particular. Just a tiny thing, like the freckle on Olaf's nose, seemed comical, and we all reeled about pointing at it and bellowing. Olaf found it equally funny. 'The spot on my nose is as large as the moon!' he screamed.

I was trying to think of something equally witty to say about Olaf's spot when I became interested in his mouth. It seemed large and dark and rimmed with big yellow teeth. As I stared, the teeth seemed to recede into the gums – all I could see was a pink circle enclosing the gullet. The mouth grew cavernous, an immense circle of blackness, and then out of it came a tiny pulse of light. At first it seemed like a mote of dust spinning in a sun-shaft, but then it flared out, expanding into a ray of white light. It was all silk and fire, the lustre of milk gilded by the raiment of the spirit. I tried to rise but fell back, overwhelmed by its pure and savage force. I turned away, shielding my eyes, but my hands were aglow with that inescapable fire. Dazzled and stricken, I was forced to bear witness…

And then I saw it, floating along a trail of pure radiance, streaming fire and phosphor, silver bird hovering in a cloud of gold – by God it was the Grail! Swooping between Olaf's lips, it rose vertically. The darkness was thrust back by the spillage of its glory. A tower of light reared over our heads and at its crown stood the sacred cup that Arthur desired. With it came this music, plunging, bright, cataracting rivers of sound, shaking and shattering the air, tumultuous and crazily joyous, as if all the larks in heaven were looping and darting and mazing their songs amid the moon and stars. Like a beckoning voice heard through deep mist, or a wafted perfume inhaled over miles of ocean, I could not trace its source, for every granule of the atmosphere was surcharged and quivering.

I jumped to my feet, shouting, 'I've found you!'

It lay poised for a while some six feet above our heads. Olaf, Skullsplitter and Eric gazed up at the divine apparition, furry mouths agape. Their eyes were faintly irate, as if the Grail had no right, in defiance of physical law, to float around unhindered. Then the chalice, tilting slightly, began to move away from the fire, over the scorched grass and stolen treasure. Hissing faintly, as though white-hot, it struck a patch of wet mist and then sailed out towards the trees and hung waiting.

Arising, I shouted farewell to my Viking comrades, for I knew that I had been singled out. Grinning drunkenly, they raised their arms and shook their clenched fists, urging me to pursue my goal. As I quickened my pace, the Grail started to draw away at the precise rate of my advance, as though it wished to lead me rather than lose me. It sailed beyond the beech clump to the place where Larkspur was grazing. There, some thirty paces ahead, it hung in the dark air like an envoy. I mounted Larkspur and urged her forward.

# 18

# BARON LONGSHANKS

T he wind blew cool on my face as Larkspur galloped towards that floating speck of light. We followed it over hill and dale, wading through rivers and saltmarshes, climbing steep hills, clashing through oakwoods and galloping along sandy bays where fierce and curling waves smashed themselves against spines of jagged rock. In a madness of exultation, I stormed and stamped over fallow fields and barren heaths. Larkspur seemed to be inspired by my obsession, sweeping along like a gale of pure force, hooves sparking off boulders, mane streaming from her arched neck.

The exultation of the chase! When the will is tempered and honed into a bright sword of purpose, pursuing a goal that entices as surely as it withdraws. It makes men ruthless and not a little mad, for such questers do not move as others. An idea – a beguiling abstract witchery – has squeezed the rind of time passing and let drip from it the juice of rapture!

That was my mood at late afternoon, as we entered a dark forest, the Grail moving more slowly, but still drifting a little ahead, like a guide waiting for a traveller to catch up. It entered a clearing where I heard the sound of trickling water and whispering leaves. Tall trees loomed on all sides like shaggy pinnacles. The Grail stopped. Slowly its glow intensified and it began to pour out streams of silver fire. They cascaded into the grass forming a pool which spread out in a star-pattern. This startled Larskpur who drew back and neighed. Sliding off my saddle, I tethered her to a tree and went to inspect on foot. Shielding my eyes, I crept towards the Grail, hovering about seven feet above the ground. Luminous rivulets still poured over the brim, trickling down and snaking outwards so that the star-points grew larger and more extended. It looked like a fierce and molten liquid, yet caused no hurt, giving off neither smoke nor heat. Only there was a certain smell in the air, vaguely musky like a rare oil or gum.

I edged closer until the stream of my breath was touched by its glow. The Grail was only one foot above me, incandescent and stationary. I stretched up on my toes, eyes averted from the stabbing glow, and reached up to grasp the chalice.

And then it went out like a snuffed candle.

Numb with disappointment, I cursed loudly, beat around the trees, stamping and grinding my teeth. It was impossible for me to sleep, and I sat up all night, brooding. When dawn flushed the sky, I realised that I still was under the thrall of the mushrooms. Things around me – trees, stones and plants – were unnaturally sharp and bright. Sounds were magnified yet blurred and accompanied by a rushing noise.

I paced around to establish my whereabouts. I was in the upper part of a narrow valley through which a stream flowed down to a flour mill and pond where ducklings played. At the entrance of the inlet, high up on a mound, was a small stone hermitage.

Mounting Larkspur, I rode down to the base of the mound, from where a flight of rock-cut steps ascended to the hermitage. These I climbed and stood before a door with heavy iron strapwork. It swung open revealing a tiny oblong cell. The stone-enfolded air made me flinch, for it bore the taint of sweat and death. And then I saw, slumped on the floor beneath the single window, the body of a knight. His helmet lay at his feet, a metal husk, and next to it was his sword. He was stretched out, still as a log, save for his hands that were tightly clenched. With his arrogant jaw and dramatic prow of a nose, he was still a handsome man, although his eyes were blood-flecked, yellow at the corners, and a long-suffered pain was stamped upon his features.

'Lancelot!' I cried. 'What is wrong?'

I stepped forward and peered closely. A terrible ochre and brown stain covered most of his armour, and part of it had crept over his right hand and stained his cheek also. It was as if a lightning bolt had frozen a flaming streak down the entire length of his body. The metal was perished and decayed: a bright and ravenous rust spreading from the links to the skin.

'Galahad,' he groaned, lifting his head a little. 'I am glad that you have come. I am enduring the last moments of this life, and I wish to confess my sins before I depart to the hereafter.'

Kneeling, I lifted his head onto my lap to ease his breathing. 'Lancelot, if it will lessen your burden, continue your story. But do not vex your conscience with unnecessary guilt. The world is a confederacy of sinners, and you are nobler than most.'

He did not seem to take in my words. His lips moved without making a sound, and then his voice came back, gasping and fragile. 'For a year, I had been deceiving Arthur – having an adulterous liaison with Queen Guinevere. When the Grail appeared, I thought I would repent by seeking out the chalice. But although I rode far and wide, my mind was not set on the mission, but on the memory of the Queen whom I had deserted. One night, I prayed that we should be re-united. The next morning, when I awoke, I found that a patch of rust had appeared on my breastplate. Gazing on the tarnished scales, I was reminded of Guinevere's hair. My thoughts flew back to her, and the more I dwelt on her face, her bodily perfection, the deeper the rust entered, the further it spread. So I tried to rid myself of this obsession by galloping hard, seeking adventures, slaying evil-doers, fasting at monasteries, but it was of no avail. For the good work I did during the day was undone at night, when I dreamed of the Queen constantly. So I would awake to cold, lonely dawns in deserted forests or barren moors, and the desire would arise in me anew. You see, Galahad, you cannot banish lust and loving from your mind. Fight it by day with promises and resolves, and at night it will creep back and taunt you. And so it was with this tenacious plague that riddled my mind and body with its incurable corruption. The more I fought it, the stronger it grew, until it blocked out the sun, and now my body is all eaten away and there is no hope.'

He began to cough. I placed my arm behind his head, forcing it up slightly. He groaned, and I bundled up my riding-cloak and pushed it behind his head as a pillow. 'Did you see the Grail?' I asked, when he had revived a little.

Lancelot nodded dimly. 'I saw a vision of it in my death-fever. I followed it to this hermitage, where I lay down. I saw it again last night, floating above my bed. This morning, when I opened my eyes, it had gone.' He gazed bleakly at his cracked, fiery hand. 'Now I am ready to die.'

I wetted his lips with a little water. 'Rest,' I said. 'You will feel better if you get this armour off.'

'I cannot get it off,' he gasped. 'Like a crab's shell, it is grafted onto my skin. The splintered metal has infected my blood, and only death can ease my agony.'

I waited, trying to soothe him as he writhed and sweated. But what can one say at such times? Any attempt to bandage suffering in language is an effontery. Physical agony will not be purchased or lessened by a string of noises, and my efforts at consolation were soon abandoned. When the sun had gone down, I left him resting and attended to Larkspur, feeding her some hay and water from the stream. When I came back, Lancelot's mouth was open as if frozen in a scream. His staring eyes were dull as sand and no air moved between his parted lips. 'Let this hermitage be his tomb,' I thought, jamming the door tight and blocking the entrance with a large stone.

The next morning I rose early and scanned the landscape. There was an inlet on the far side of the valley, hitherto concealed in shadow. On the shoulder of a steep slope, I made out a castle with a towering keep, greeny-black in colour and flying pennons adorned with eagles and doves. A premonitory shiver ran down my back, for I realised that I had been led to this place by design rather than by accident.

Suddenly I was back in the region of Cambridge, at the edge of Wandlebury Forest, listening to the words of the idiot youth – he whom I had rewarded with the gift of a knife. Fragments of his narrative strummed faintly in my mind like notes from an improvised tune. I should seek 'a castle covered all over black and green, flying pennons adorned with eagles and doves…' What else had the boy said? I racked my brain until further words returned. If I hoped to find the Grail, he said, I should enter the chapel within the fortifications, pick up the cross and strike the wall with it thrice. The instructions seemed nonsensical, yet I had enacted grosser follies while intent on this quest, so I made up my mind to try.

I rode up the slope of the hill to the castle. It was a massive building with a high central keep, the upper part of which was adorned with ranged shields upheld by the busts of fighting men. There was a moat where swans preened themselves and lilies grew thick. Immediately I saw the reason for the green on black – clumps of emerald moss clinging to dark stonework. The drawbridge was down and I let myself through on horseback. A steward ran forward and shouted a greeting. I asked if he might take Larkspur and lead her to the drinking trough. Thanking him, I asked him the way to the chapel, which he told me backed the refectory.

I found it to be a small building with pointed windows. Entering, I saw a magnificent altar-cross, all studded with beryls and rubies, lying between a pair of silver candlesticks. I went up the aisle and picked it up, using both hands for it was very heavy. Heaving it upon my shoulders, I swung it hard against the wall, striking it three times, and then I heard the voice of a priest cry out, 'Vandal! Blasphemer! Cease your devilish trade!'

'I'm looking for the Grail,' I explained.

Not surprisingly, my words cut no ice. The priest insisted on taking me to see Baron Longshanks, the hereditary lord of the castle and surrounding estates. I agreed, for I had been behaving rashly under the influence of the mushrooms. A more diplomatic approach might help.

I was escorted to the Baron, a big squarish man with a skin as white as cheese. He was wearing a long primrose gown, making his complexion appear very sickly. He had a flabby, intelligent face, with hound-jowls and hard, unblinking eyes that suggested fairness and obstinacy in equal measure. He listened to my explanation with pursed lips.

'Normally I'd throw you out, as one does thieves or interlopers, but as you claim to be from Arthur's court, I will give you a hearing. For I actually do know of you, Sir Galahad, yes. Did you not gain a reputation through something unsual? God's bones! I remember – *sitting on a chair*! That astounds me. Not that I wish to slight your name, sir, but did you know that, years back, knights had to stretch their valour to the utmost. Yes, they had to defend castles, vanquish villains and ride to the ends of the earth in order to gain a reputation. But to you, it seems to have come far easier.'

Eyes slitted, teeth bared, I endured this and replied with savage patience.

'Baron Longshanks, call it what you will, a wile of fate, a trick of destiny, history's mischief, but sometimes lesser deeds prevail over acts over acts of valour and daring. And that is how it has been with me. I *have* fought in bloody wars, won jousting tournaments, besieged castles of infidels, vanquished countless tyrants and ogres, and yet *none* talk of these dauntless deeds – all they remember is that farback day when I sat upon a chair.'

Baron Longshanks gestured at a servant who was standing at attention by the door. The young lad came forward holding a stately chair with vine leaves carved around the legs. He set it down behind me and moved away.

'Be seated, Galahad!' ordered Longshanks. 'So that I shall actually witness this deed of reknown.'

Pleased at his jest, the baron smiled, and I, with not a little weariness, made a low growling sound – though I wished to be polite, I could not bludgeon a drop of laughter out. Instead I stared at the chair as if I had received insult from it.

'Surely,' said Longshanks, 'you need to rest after riding so long and hard.'

That being true, I did relent and sit down gratefully on the (exceedingly comfortable) chair but that was not the end. For Longshanks did not want his jest to die. So he made a pretence of kneeling at my feet, throwing up his hands, exclaiming, 'Glory! Glory! How beautifully that knight sitteth!' and creeping around with a awestruck gaze, begging me to stand up and sit down again, saying how he was struck by the wonder and beauty of the way I fixed myself on that bit of wood.

What could I do? Mustering every ounce of resolve, I hammered out a tempered-steel smile. That soothed and flattered Longshanks, although inside I was a boiling mass of devils. Sodding Oddbods! Jokes are not wines that improve with the years but more like cheeses or eggs; they grow more stinking and fearsome with the telling over again. But I had to allow the baron his bit of pranking before I could lead him back to the nub of my enquiry: the search for holy treasure.

'This boy I met in Wandlebury Forest, he pictured this castle so well that I was able to pick it out, even though I had not planned on coming.'

Baron Longshanks moved over to the window, rested his hand on his chin, thought a little and then turned back to me.

'You claim that this story, that had my castle in it, was told to you by an idiot youth,' he said. 'What was his name?'

'I do not know, but he could not have lived far from the village of Sawston in Cambridge.'

The Baron nodded. 'That would have been my nephew, Albertus Longshanks. My brother brought him here on several occasions, and Albertus was forever wandering, exploring odd corners and making up fantastic tales of knights, dragons and giants. Sometimes I enjoyed his foolish prattle, but more often it stirred in me a longing for the commonplace.' He gave me a bold stare and added. 'You should know better, Sir Galahad, than to believe the chatter of the afflicted.'

'When you are looking for the Grail,' said I, 'it is necessary to keep an open mind.'

'Credulous might be a better word.'

'I intended no damage to your chapel. I was merely recalling some instructions.'

The Baron paused. Eyeing me severely, he said, 'Tell me again the elements of the story.'

'After I struck the cross thrice against the chapel wall,' I told him, 'I was supposed to see a black man, who would offer me a drink out of two cups, a wooden and a brass. If I drank out of the wooden one, a swan with a chain would appear, and, if out of the brass, a lion arrayed in purple.'

The Baron rose to his feet. 'Let us explore the chapel.'

We went down the stairs and out into the courtyard. The baron briskly made towards the chapel. Inside, he led me to a window at the back of the altar. 'What do you think of this?' he asked.

It was a painted-glass window, wheel-headed in design, containing all the story motifs – a black man, swan, lion, two-cups – in the various lead-framed sections.

'This is obviously the basis of the boy's story,' said I, 'but what is the general meaning?'

'It is an old window, illustrating a legend,' replied the Baron rather warily.

I pointed to some letters, cross-hatched and unclear, also written into the window. 'It looks there as if mason's marks have been worked into the painted glass. Have you any like these in the building?'

He spread both hands in an expansive flourish. 'Look around and see.'

Baron Longshanks left the chapel, saying that he would return later. I set about the investigation. For hours I pored over the markings on the chapel walls, most of which were recent, but at last I found a fragment of ancient work. I ran my hands down it, to see if there were any loose parts. When I found a block that gave under pressure, I looked it over thoroughly for the mason's marks. Eureka! I found some exactly matching the window-letters. Using a dagger, I scraped away the pinkish mortar and eased the stone out. Then I put my hand in the wall and explored the rubble filling. My fingers touched and grasped a metal object, drawing it out in a shower of powdered stone. It was a rough bronze chalice, very old, but substantial, and of average craftsmanship. There was little decoration save some lozenge-shaped marks and beading lower down. I rapped its surface; there was a distinct ring, indicating sound workmanship.

I held it up, smiling to myself, then Baron Longshanks entered. 'What have you there?' he asked.

'See for yourself.'

I handed over my find. He looked a little taken aback, frowning as he clasped the coarse metal. When he spoke his voice was halting and restrained. 'Is this the chalice?' he asked.

'It had better be,' I told him. 'For I am getting sorely tired with searching.'

The Baron narrowed his eyes. His breathed out heavily and pursed his lips. I could see he was trying to phrase his thoughts tactfully. 'We have plenty of vessels similar to this,' he announced.

The words sank into the depths of my soul like cold wet stones, dousing delight. After countless perilous gallopings and hairbreadth escapes, I was again a trampled rat, a hornless snail, a sprawled and bleeding Icarus! Meadmore was right; one might as well be a drunkard, effort being so tardily rewarded. 'What!' said I. 'Surely it is not possible.'

'If you will accompany me…'

The Baron led me out of the chapel into an annex. Passing through a room with groined walls and trefoil-headed windows, he entered a refectory with a pantry at the back where he pointed to a high shelf where a double row of Grails blazed and sang like hardened flames. All were made of bronze and had identical lozenge patterns around the rims and coarse beading at the bases.

'How did you come by all these chalices?' said I.

'A distant ancestor of mine bought them from a Phoenician trader, a man named Joseph of Arimithea.'

'Was not that the Joseph who was the uncle to Jesus of Nazareth?'

The Baron shrugged. 'Possibly. He put down his occupation as a Grail-seller.'

'But how did that one Grail come to be walled inside the chapel?'

The Baron gave me a troubled glance. He looked at the floor and replied with pained sincerity. 'I have not been entirely honest with you, Sir Galahad.'

'Is that so?' said I grimly.

'This Joseph,' the Baron explained, 'told my forefather that the coming years would increase the value of Holy Grails. He recommended that one of his descendants should secrete one in a hideout, keeping the rest as replacements should ever the hidden one become lost or damaged. He also urged that a special code should be attached to it – something mystical and high-sounding, he said – so that whoever found it should believe that he had discovered something unique. Inaccessibility increases the value of relics, he said. So naturally, when I raised the chapel, I employed a mason to wall in the Grail along with all sorts of pictographs and clues. Now my nephew, Albertus, was drawn to the chapel. Each day he'd explore it, weaving stories around the pictures and designs.'

'Why did you not tell me in the first place?'

'The work was done over twenty years ago, and I had myself forgotten the code. This made me all the more intrigued to see whether you could interpret it.'

I felt so frustrated that I could have butted my head against a wall then buried it in a mound of pig-dung. What was I to do? The Holy Grail was not a unique relic, only one of many identical vessels – clearly there had been an industry in such artefacts.

'You have given me much to think about – not to say vex over,' I told Longshanks, 'so you must pardon me if I take some time on my own, to brood and think things out, before I come back to you with a proposition.'

Leaving Longshanks, I wandered around the castle, confused and dejected. I climbed the battlements and looked out over the rolling moors where the wind swirled and chased cloud-shadows. On the lower slopes, the peasants were out with oxen and ploughs. Against the outline of the massive hillside, it was as if they were insect-men working on the body of some giant dun-colored beast, raking and tidying its powdery hide. Somehow their lives seemed pre-ordained, complete. None cared about Grails and ornate fancies, only the long diurnal rhythm of hoeing, seeding and harvesting. Their lives did not allow for myths or fancies, save late at night when the real work had finished, and they could allow themselves a tale or two to divert their children. Only Arthur could live by dreams, grazing the surface of legends and tapestries, thinking he would discover more about life – a central source, a finite principle – in those very things that are most distant from it.

The wind dropped; the sun shivered behind a gathering gloom of cloud. I descended the battlements and crossed the courtyard. Finally I returned to the chapel. The light was shrinking tight around the lowering orb, throwing gloomy nets of shade across the benches and carved stones.

The Grail – the chalice found lodged in the wall – was placed on a small stone table, below the painted window, and its outline was strangely definite. It seemed to have drained whatever light remained, and it stood out, dramatic as a white bird skimming across a lake of pitch. Beguiled by this play of fancy, I moved towards it, noting with a shock that the goblet – by intervention, infernal or divine – had become filled with liquid.

The surface of the goblet was alive, a trapped circle of sweetness. It was royal-red, bubbling slightly and it exuded a scent of wine spiced with nutmeg and cinnamon. The smell infused the caverns of my senses, and it seemed that I had no choice. It had been a hard day, filled with death and questing, and I had wracked brain and limb.

So I lifted it to my lips and quaffed it in a single gulp.

How did I find the bedchamber Baron Longshanks had put aside for my use? Drunkenness often pitches knights into moats and cesspits, but on happier occasions it can bring out a certain native wit for navigation, guiding me up a tortuous flight of unguarded steps to a snug stone chamber, with a window the size of a breastplate and a swansdown bed covered all over with quilts of fur and wool. For that was the room in which I awoke. Yes, I had slept a full, deep sleep, secure as a trout in a lake, the tiny quantity of wine having entered my head potently. And the sleep brought with it a dream.

I was a child again, wandering in the fields and farms around Dykesyat. It was high summer. The hedges and ditches drowsed in a haze of misty vapour through which flitted winged insects and mazy cabbage whites. I had just visited a favourite spot, two huge old oaks called Gog and Magog, set at the foot of the tall, terraced hill, where Dylfric had established his oratory, and on the lower slopes of which the monks grew vines. But my mood was sad.

Standing beneath the boughs of these green-haired patriarchs, I was thinking about my mother, lately consiged to the earth. The funeral had been rigid and ordered: long-faced rows of relatives; masses of strewn flowers; and my father, clad in sable silk, standing over the coffin, rigid as steeple, as he swallowed back that smarting core – that which needed to sink its sorrow down into the very earth that was openly accepting the one whom he loved. And I thought: *this is what my questing truly is* – not searching for a Grail, but fleeing that stalking archer of souls, that shadowy hunter that pursues men through all their dreams and strategies and never – never – misses his mark!

As this thought occurred, I heard a voice pierce the frond of my dream. Not a grand, sonorous voice, crying 'Go forth!' or 'Try harder – quicken thy resolve, Sir Galahad!' but a whispering, gentle undertone, like a coaxing nursemaid or friendly teacher.

This voice dared to suggest that the luminous vessel – the true 'Holy Grail' – was not meant for the likes of Lancelor or myself. Composed of fire, phosphor and streaming incense, our souls were too tainted to encompass it. We had enjoyed the brief privilege of confusing and evasive glimpses of it, yes, but that was all all. They were akin to crumbs dropped from the celestial table or the Divinity showing compassion for hopeless clods!

The idea did not offend, for I had never hankered after purity – not after my initiation at Cerne Abbas. No, it settled in my head like a perching angel – yet there was an issue still to be resolved. Why did that spiritual Grail – the one of fire and flowing substance – lead me from the Viking camp to Lancelot's hermitage and then to Longshanks' castle? Surely not to pointlessly taunt me. No, being a chalice of compassion, the vessel had guided me, so that I should first drink the 'wine' of self-knowledge and then claim a receptacle more befitting my earthly, practical nature – one of Baron Longshanks's not-so-holy but solid and reliably crafted Grails!

By my calling, I was a noble and valiant knight to whom the term 'falsehood' was wholly vile, but even so, if my mission were to be deemed a success, I would have to conceal such knowledge at all costs. Throwing on my surcoat and hose, I quit the bedchamber and found the lord of the castle supervising the grooms in the stable.

'Look Baron Longshanks, I have struck a problem here. You see, I was sent by King Arthur to find *the* Holy Grail – not a whole set! What can I say? You have far too many holy vessels here for a knight's comfort. It makes a mockery of the whole quest.'

The Baron gave me a round-eyed stare. 'I am not to be accounted for the whims of kings.'

'I realise that,' said I, 'but I cannot say how grateful I would be, were you to dispose of your remarkable collection of chalices.'

Baron Longshanks drew himself up like one affronted. 'Sir Galahad, you fail to appreciate that my Grails are family heirlooms. They have served us well, being hardy and enduring receptacles, guaranteed not to shatter, bend or break. You cannot expect me to cast them out.'

'Why not put them in a sack and throw them down a well?' said I. 'That way, if you urgently need need one, you can always haul them up. Should you agree, I swear by the Holy Rood that I shall replace each goblet with a genuine tin beaker of advanced design, drawn from the mines of Priddy on the Mendips.'

# 19

# THE RETURN

The following morning, the bronze Grail packed in my saddlebag, I took breakfast with Baron Longshanks, who had agreed to conceal his Grail-collection, and made ready to leave. Feeling stout-humoured, I rode Larkspur out of the gate, taking the track that ran south-west over the moors and mountains of Cumbria. After a day and night of journeying, I passed the huts and storage pits of the rude settlement at Penrith. A tall hill loomed before me, rising up from the shore of a broad lake tufted with green islets. I climbed up to the ridge and saw a cairn and milepost. Before I could check my bearings and begin the descent, Larkspur shuddered to a halt and neighed. I stopped and waited, hearing a thunder of mighty hooves.

Over the brow of the hill charged four red and white oxen dragging behind an ugly horned thing – the head of Herne!

'Whoa! Whoa!' shouted Herne. The oxen stopped.

'You're still alive!' I exclaimed. 'Congratulations.'

'Galahad,' said he, 'I thought I told you that I cannot die. I am one of the immortals.' He grinned.

'Yes, but surely, it is a poor life without a body.'

'On the contrary,' replied Herne, 'it is a most excellent life. You should try it, Galahad.'

'I don't know, Herne. I'm more squeamish about these things.'

Herne laughed, a strong and jubilant bass. 'Since I last saw you, Galahad, I have had a most wonderful time. I have been to the Abbey of Croyland and seen Guthlac's shrine. And then the oxen dragged me into Berkshire where I saw the great white horse carved on the hill. Then I was pulled over the Welsh mountains where I saw a stone that bled if you struck it with a hammer, and then I was drawn by the beasts right the way down to Cornwall – a most lovely land! No trees, wild cliffs, sandy beaches and many quaint old pixies and fishermen. I went to Land's End, Lyonesse and visited Castle Dinas and St Michael's Mount. I met the giant Bolster and the Padstow Obby Oss and we all drank mead together on Brown Willy. O Galahad, believe me, Britain is a fabulous land when you get to see it. Snowdon, Cheddar Caves, Gordale Scar, the Great Hole of Blaunogbonywygelly – these are most marvellous sights! Faith, had I hands, I would write a book and call it, 'The Beauties of Britain'.'

'You might be able to dictate it to a priest or scribe,' said I.

'Should I write it in Latin?'

'I do not know, Herne. My learning is modest, but I recommend that you should hire an artist. Pictures are very important if you intend to compose a book.'

'Is that right, Galahad?'

'Yes, Herne. Did you know there are manuscripts in which you can paint and draw around the margins?'

This insight delighted Herne. His head, buoyant as a salmon, sprang a full foot above the ground and the points of his horns glowed like May blossom. Clearly the notion of book-making had got him all hotted-up.

'Truly, Galahad? You are refined, knowing that sort of thing.'

'Well, Herne, you're civilized, too – saving all those prisoners!'

'Is that right, Galahad?'

'Yes, Herne. Did you know there are manuscripts wherein you can paint and draw around the margins?'

This insight delighted Herne. His head, buoyant as a salmon, sprang a full foot above the ground and the points of his horns glowed like May blossom. Clearly the notion of book-making had got him all hotted-up.

'Truly, Galahad? You are refined, knowing that sort of thing.'

'Well, Herne, you're civilized, too – saving those prisoners!'

Herne's head touched down to earth. His shrubby eyebrows bushed up as if I were talking of matters unknown. So I recalled to him how he had quenched the Wicker Man and enabled the escape.

'Were you present, Galahad? I did not see you.'

'You galloped off an instant later.'

'Well,' Herne explained, 'I was in a hurry to see Strangwell Spout.'

'Strangwell Spout! Is he that fellow who talks incessantly?'

'No, Galahad, it is a waterfall!'

'A waterfall!'

'Yes, I find the sight of water pounding itself to atoms soothing. It does a terrible violence to its body, then miraculously heals the commotion, drawing its corpuscles together and flowing on down to the sea.'

'Indeed,' said I, 'it has a quick-changing, ever-adapting nature. Like yourself, Herne, acting instantly and saving those prisoners from a dreadful fate.'

'It was nothing, Galahad,' he replied. 'It was always beholden on me to put out fires in Wandlebury, and I still try to keep such things under control, unlike the Druids who set alight to everything that moves. Now, how stand things with you – did you find the Grail?'

I nodded. 'It is a bronze cup. Not very impressive. But it should satisfy Arthur for a while.'

Herne creased his brow in agreement. Then he closed his eyes, as if summoning power from within, and his horns twitched a little. I sensed he was trying to broach something that irked him. 'Galahad,' he declared, 'I want to ask you a personal question. Is my countenance alarming to look upon? You see, I have been thinking I'd like to marry and settle down.'

A painfully long pause. I cleared my throat, bit my lip, scratched my chin, finally replying. 'Nobody's sweetheart is ugly, Herne, and I think that you have a forceful face.'

Herne smiled showing a row of bark-brown teeth. 'How reassuring you are, Galahad. You see, I am vexed by the behaviour of milkmaids. Whenever the oxen draw up beside them, and I try to exchange a pleasantry or two, they scream and flee.'

'Frivolous creatures, women,' I muttered. 'They love to squawk and scatter on seeing a rugged stranger.'

Herne asked gravely. 'Do you think they are afeared for their virginity?'

I pondered this and replied cautiously. 'If you do not mind me saying so, Herne, in your present bodiless state, rape of any sort would present a formidable problem. No, I think you are merely the subject of a glorious tease.'

Herne nodded approval at my consolatory warblings. Taking deep breaths, he hung out an oakleaf-shaped tongue and panted.

'Do you want me to get you a drink, Herne?'

'I would be obliged, Galahad. And there is another little thing you could do for me. Getting dragged along by oxen, although passably exciting, is not the seemliest way to see the land. Furthermore, a great deal of mud and grit has got stuck to my face, impairing my vision, and I would be most grateful if you could dunk my head in a trough and give it a good soak.'

'Of course, Herne,' said I.

Herne's head was crushingly heavy – it might have been a chunk of solid rock. I knelt down and unclipped it from the harness straps. Then, taking it by the antler-points, I strained and hauled it down to the nearest drinking trough, which was set beside a cascade some distance below the stone-piled summit. Then I pushed it in the water, using the antlers as a kind of handle to swill it around; mud and blood floated up to the surface.

When I heaved the head out, the eyes were restored to their normal healthy fire-red colour and his skin was no longer mud-brown but clear pale green. All in all he looked in fair condition.

'There, you look hale and handsome again,' I told him.

'Thank you, Galahad,' he replied. 'No one could call me vain, but I do appreciate an occasional immersion.'

Now I had to carry Herne's head to the top and rein it to the oxen. I deemed it time he was setting off. Although an agreeable companion, a pathos clung about Herne that sapped my spirit. A madness too. He was only a head and yet was happier than he had ever been in the depths of Wandlebury Forest. Had he willed himself never to assess, to take stock, of what he lacked and its possible consequences? Or was it that travel – being borne swiftly from place to place by those stampeding oxen – created in him a perpetual rush of pleasure that stopped him from looking inward? This caused a nervous hesitancy on my part. You see, Herne's booming heartiness was twinned with such an appalling handicap that I could not be open. At all costs I wished to avoid broaching any matter of what physical intimacy he was likely to achieve. I did not want to tell him frankly that his present existence, however fruitful a turn it might take, was not likely to be beset by romantic entanglements.

So, wearily, I dragged the enormous smiling cranium up the stony slope, resting at intervals and telling him of my adventures when, about half-way up, I met an old white-haired man, who was staring into a pond with a pail beside him.

'What are you doing?' I enquired.

'Gathering leeches?' he replied.

'Have you been doing it long?'

'Galahad,' groaned Herne, 'do not waste time engaging that old man in conversation. He is ugly, boring and foolish. Get me up the hill.'

'We are sharp today,' said I. 'We must have slept in the knifebox.'

'I do not like leeches, Galahad. They are horrible blood-suckers and I do not desire to look upon them anymore.'

'Herne, you're full of small complaints no baby dies of.'

'Get me up the hill. You can talk to him afterwards.'

'Alright Herne, have your way. Goodbye leech-gatherer, and I wish you luck on your travels.'

The leech-gatherer did not respond. Instead he grinned. Then, bowing down, he did a most surprising thing. Stiffly raising the pail above his shoulders, with ritual solemnity he inverted it, tipping the contents over his head.

I drew back with a sick gasp. 'Why do you do that?'

The sight had the allure of the truly ghastly. Why do abominations quicken our interest? I could have easily have turned my back but instead I stared with foul fascination.

Oily green, brown-speckled worms slithered and frothed mucus over his eyes, nose and cheeks. As they moved, their small white teeth left Y-shaped wounds, like those made by certain short swords. What made it more appalling was that the leech-gatherer was now actually grinning. The worms were bulbed out with his blood and still sucking fiercely. Whereupon he let out a series of loud, ecstatic cries, and began to hoarsely pant.

Exhaling one final groan of pleasure, he collapsed and rolled over in the grass, mumbling 'Lovely! Lovely!', and then he lay still, cold and trembling, the leeches having filled themselves to capacity.

'Move on, Galahad!' urged Herne angrily. 'Have you not seen enough revolting Cumbrian customs for one day? Will you next be asking me to accompany you to their dung-eating banquets or their suicidal crag-dancing ceremonies. I tell you people up here are more dangerous and mad than the Druids, and I think it must be owing to the water they drink, for it is full of lead and copper, too much of which renders men witless!'

'You are right, Herne. The man is not fit for decent society.'

Lugging Herne's head, I climbed up to the summit of the beacon, to where I afterwards brought the oxen and began to harness up the horns.

'Where will you be going next?' I asked Herne.

'I think,' he replied, 'I would like to visit the Lake District. But what worries me is – do I have to pass through Sherwood Forest on the way? Trees, you see, still vex me no end.'

'You will have to get use to that, Herne, but no, you are still far north of Sherwood. However, these allergies need to be kept under firm control, else your mental and moral health may be undermined.'

'And what of you, Galahad?'

'It's back to Camelot and drinking for me.'

I paused, securing the harness, to send Herne off, when I heard a loud voice which seemed to be coming from on high. 'Galahad! Galahad!' it cried.

'Look!' exclaimed Herne. 'There is a great bird up in the sky. He is signalling to you.'

I gazed up. A vast bird-form was hovering on the morning breeze. It was so large that I thought it might be a creature of fable, a winged dragon or an angel who had strayed out of heaven into the lower regions. But as it got closer, I could tell it was none of those – no, it was a machine of queer design, with big straight, wide boards sticking out of it. The figure of a man was outlined against the strange shape. As it swooped low, I saw a glint of golden hair and ruddy cheeks and recognised it was King Bladud. But he had undergone a most extraordinary transformation. He had discarded his orginal flying device for a thing that beggar'd description. I could now see how it was made. Of cloth and wood, it had two sets of wings, the smaller at the back, sprouting a wind-rudder, and between the wings a little perch, or nest, in which he sat operating levers and strings. Strapped in tightly, he sported a long feathery moustache and was clad in a tunic of sheepskin turned inside out. He had a tight little leather cap on his head and gaped at me through strange goggles.

'Galahad,' he cried, circling overhead. 'Excuse me for addressing you from this height, but I have important news from the south, and I cannot fly lower and risk pranging my pride and joy. So listen closely – my daughter Catherine wishes to see you. She has told me how there has been much fighting. Arthur is at war with his half-brother Modred and all the knights are being called back.'

'I have heard nothing,' said I shaken.

Herne looked at me. His eyes glinted and emerald lips quivered. 'You have been too long hunting Grails,' he said.

# ❧ 20 ❧

# THE LAST BATTLE

The nearer events in time, the more difficult they are to set down. The present is wide and open, almost featureless. It has in it a thousand small, unnoticed things which leap up and and beset one, creating their own echoes and accidents down the path of time. Up close, details overwhelm and loom larger than they should. We are presented with things we must grasp at or let go, with no idea of the import they may accrue. The past, by comparison, is like a path whose corners and windings have distinct stones and landmarks by which one can find one's way about. It is less crowded, in that memory has buried much, and thus it is here, near the end of my story, I forsake detail and present only the bare outline. Besides, there is pain in the retelling, in the spelling out of foibles and failings, and I am no author, but a knight who has achieved nothing save a sketchy contentment in middle age.

Arthur in trouble. Rumours of war – his half-brother Modred seeking the throne. I had to return to Camelot and find out how things stood.

Through driving rain, I galloped, sleeping in snatches, pulling up over freezing Penine passes and black gritstone moors, then south to Sarum and westwards to Camelot. My heart was glad to see that green-gold country with all the leaves aflame in high summer and the loamy earth bearing fruit. I skirted the base of the camp and entered the knobbly hill country behind Sutton Montis.

Soon I saw the walls and parapets of Camelot. But when I entered, there was no sound in the great courtyard, no trimly bearded squires, no stewards or serving wenches, and all the shields in the hall were gone. Empty stables. Hollow rooms. The Round Table with all the names of the knights, my friends, but none there to greet me. I sat down on the Siege Perilous and stared at my name as if it belonged to another.

'Sir Galahad, you are back.'

It was Arthur's servant, elderly Hugh Pandulph. He looked drained and sad. I asked him what had happened.

'There has been a great battle,' he replied. 'At Camlan.'

My chest tightened. I left him and rode away to the east, until I came to the place he had named. The valley was wedge-shaped and entered at the narrow end by crossing a bridge where two streams mingled their floods.

A rough stone post, on which had been carved a crude sun-face, marked the meeting of the ways. A woman was sitting beside it, one slim hand laid against the coarse granite like a petal. She was dark-eyed with groomed hair and a hint of rose in her cheeks.

'You are too late, Galahad,' Catherine said. 'It is all over. I came here to tell you, so that we might renew our friendship in the face of so much slaughter?'

'Who won the battle?'

Catherine shivered and looked down. 'There was no victor, only the dead and vanquished.'

'Did any survive?'

'One knight only. He hangs around the battlefield like a demented thing.'

'You waited to give me this message?'

Catherine shook her head. 'No, to see you again. You told me that you valued me above all other women. I regret the price but a new die has been cast. Galahad, the old order has passed away.'

I halted Larkspur and dismounted. Catherine came across from the bridge and took me in her arms. Naturally as one sways with the wind, I yielded to the soft pressure of her greeting. It was if a bridge of understanding had grown of its own accord across the gap of separation.

'The vision of Camelot is stained and bloodied,' she whispered, as she held me. 'O Galahad, there are no longer any laws or codes by which you must abide. You must rebuild on what there is left.' Drawing her head back, she gave a gentle, grave look, adding. 'And I can show you how to do that. Unless you prefer to dwell upon past desolation rather than future hope.'

'When I first met you, I was urging you on too fast,' said I. 'Now you are drawing up plans, before I know anything.'

She gestured emptily down the valley. 'It is all down there, waiting for you.'

'I will see it for myself,' I told her.

Catherine lowered her eyes. 'I will wait here. What little I have seen is enough.'

I left Catherine swearing that I would return shortly. In my haste, I rode across a field of corn, trampling down the ripening ears, crushing and breaking golden heads and stalks. As I rode, I came across certain trophies. A spear wrapped in white bliant lying amid the poppies and flattened grain, a triple-grooved sword, a sheath of red deerskin and an immense banner showing the black cobra of Modred on a scarlet silk background.

Dismounting, I knelt and touched the standard of Arthur's adversary. Then I became aware of another's shadow. Looking about me, I saw a knight with a foolish, familiar countenance and a small querulous mouth. His inflamed face confronted me with the same glazed stare. It might have been the end of the world, the last judgement trumpetting from the skies, and his attitude would have been the same: one of slightly puzzled petulance but never of genuine grief or regret.

'Faith Galahad, what a bloody spectacle! All dead, all of them, and I have still got the thirst.'

'Did you fight Meadmore?'

'Fight Galahad! Did I fight?' His blotched eyes glinted as he slurred and drawled. 'Yes, indeed, I fought like ten dragons. I killed Modred and his henchman with my bare hands. I strangled oafs seven foot tall and hacked the heads off charging foot soldiers. I repelled the cavalry with my basilisk glance. I danced like a demon among the carnage of my foes. I was the pride of the field, Galahad, the pride of the field.'

I countered the lie, saying. 'You did not fight, Meadmore. Like myself, you missed the battle, and, if you had fought, you would have been too drunk to discriminate between friend and foe.'

Meadmore let out a dull groan and slumped down on his haunches. 'I did fight valiantly, Galahad,' he slurred. 'Up here,' he tapped his aching forehead, 'I fought an honest battle if nowhere else.'

'And do you know who the winner of your battle was?' I picked up an empty pitcher of wine and shook it in front of his nose. 'Yes, it beats you every time, doesn't it Meadmore?'

'A far kinder opponent than some I could name,' he retorted. 'It does no violence to the body, only gently dulls the mind.'

I left Meadmore rambling. I had admonished him, yet knew he was not to blame for anything. A man should not be condemned for choosing life instead of death or drunkenness instead of sobriety. For a drunkard has a virtue of his own, in that his ways are not beset or ordered by others. He does not go forth to march and die like a soldier. He shows a wilful separateness – dedication to an overarching need – that defines him as a man. And often he makes easy, pleasant company. One can breathe freely and take stock of oneself in the presence of a laggard. The fiercely virtuous, on the other hand, tire and exhaust with their rigour.

I decided to proceed on foot and explore the deeper field. After a while I came across the bodies, black and bloated, lying amid the rustling wands of gold: hundreds of them – an immense tonnage of plate, link and hauberk. Already the rain had tarnished the breastplates, joints and divides. Already the pageant of the earth had dimmed their glory. Already the wheeling sky had turned them over in the dust. I sensed that time had isolated me, the last of the knights, the one left back after the others had passed on.

I searched among the bodies, faces of clay splashed with coagulated blood. Little white specks lay on their eyes where flies had pitched. Their mouths were brown and some were open as if they were silently speaking to the curve of the sky. Every so often, the long wind would sweep over them, then fade out and lie down like a weary warrior. The sweet smell of heat and death trembled amid the roots and odours of growing things. Golden fields, blue sky, the sun bearing down like a lion, and all around the prone harvest of the reaper.

When I found Arthur, I was glad that he still looked fair, though his face too was darkened by putrefaction. His standard-bearer had draped his body with the great red and gold dragon of his father, Uther, which had braved many a wind of war. I touched his hand, but it was as if he had never been alive, so absolute was its repose. The fingers of a dead man, pointless and empty, like a broken twig lying on a path. With a pain that plucked deep into my soul's core, I took out the bronze Grail, pressed it into his hand and rode back over the field of gold and towards the figure of a woman waiting by a bridge.